The Cave Man

The Cave Man

Edgar Rice Burroughs

ÆGYPAN PRESS

The Cave Man was serialized in *The All-Story Magazine* in 1917.

The Cave Man
A publication of
ÆGYPAN PRESS

www.aegypan.com

I

KING BIG FIST

*W*aldo Emerson Smith-Jones, scion of the aristocratic house of the John Alden Smith-Jones of Boston, clambered up the rocky face of the precipitous cliff with the agility of a monkey.

His right hand clasped the slim fingers of his half-naked mate, assisting her over the more dangerous or difficult stretches.

At the summit the two turned their faces back toward the sea. Beyond the gently waving forest trees stretched the broad expanse of the shimmering ocean. In the foreground, upon the bosom of a tiny harbor, lay a graceful yacht — a beautiful toy it looked from the distance of the cliff top.

For the first time the man obtained an unobstructed view of the craft. Before, when they first had discovered it, the boles of the trees had revealed it but in part.

Now he saw it fully from stem to stern with all its well-known graceful lines standing out distinctly against the deep blue of the water.

The shock of recognition brought and involuntary exclamation from his lips. The girl looked quickly up into his face.

"What is it, Thandar?" she asked. "What do you see?"

"The yacht!" he whispered. "It is the *Priscilla* — my father's. He is searching for me."

"And you wish to go?"

For some time he did not speak — only stood there gazing at the distant yacht. And the young girl at his side remained quite motionless and silent, too, looking upon his face with a look of dumb misery upon her own.

Quickly through the man's mind was running the gamut of his past. He recalled his careful and tender upbringing — the time, the money, the fond pride that had been expended upon his education. He thought of the result — the narrow-minded weakling egoist; the pusillanimous coward that had been washed from the deck of a passing steamer upon the sandy beach of this savage, forgotten shore.

And yet it had been love, solicitous and tender, that had prompted his parents to their misguided efforts. He was their only son. They were doubtless grieving for him. They were no longer young, and in their declining years it appeared to him a pathetic thing that they should be robbed of the happiness which he might bring them by returning to the old life.

But could he ever return to the bookish existence that once had seemed so pleasant?

Had not these brief years into which had been crowded so much of wild, primitive life made impossible a return to the narrow, self-centered existence? Had it not taught him that there was infinitely more in life than ever had been written into the dry and musty pages of books?

It had taught him to want life at first hand — not through the proxy of the printed page. It and — Nadara. He glanced toward the girl.

Could he give her up? No! A thousand times no!

He read in her face the fear that lurked in her heart. No, he could not give her up. He owed to her all that he possessed of which he was most proud — his mighty physique, his newfound courage, his woodcraft, his ability to cope, primitively, with the primitive world . . . her savage world which he had learned to love.

No, he could not give her up; but — what? His gaze lingered upon her sweet face. Slowly there sank into his understanding something of the reason for his love of this wild, half-savage cave girl other than the primitive passion of the sexes.

He saw now not only the physical beauty of her face and figure, but the sweet, pure innocence of her girlishness, and most of all, all the wondrous tenderness of her love of him that was mirrored in her eyes.

To remain and take her as his mate after manner and customs of her own people would reflect no shame upon himself or her; but was she not deserving of the highest honor that it lay within his power to offer at the altar of her love?

She — his wonderful Nadara — must become his through the most solemn and dignified ceremony that civilized man had devised. What the young woman of his past life demanded was none too good for her.

Again the girl voiced her question.

"You wish to go?"

"Yes, Nadara," he replied, "I must go back to my own people — and you must go with me."

Her faced lighted with pleasure and happiness as she heard his last words; but the expression was quickly followed by one of doubt and fear.

"I am afraid," she said; "but if you wish it I will go."

"You need not fear, Nadara. None will harm you by word or deed while Thandar is with you. Come, let us return to the sea and the yacht before she sails."

Hand in hand they retraced their steps down the steep cliff, across the little valley toward the forest and the sea.

Nadara walked very close to Thandar, her hand snuggled in his and her shoulder pressed tightly against his side, for she was afraid of the new life among the strange creatures of civilization.

At the far side of the valley, just before one enters the forest, there grows a thick jungle of bamboo — really but a narrow strip, not more than a hundred feet through at its greatest width; but so dense as to quite shut out from any view any creature even a few feet within its narrow; gloomy avenues.

Into this the two plunged, Thandar in the lead, Nadara close behind him, stepping exactly in his footprints — an involuntary concession to training, for there was no need here either of deceiving a pursuer, or taking advantage of easier going. The trail was well-marked and smooth-beaten by many a padded pad.

It wound erratically, following the line of least resistance — it forked, and there were other trails which entered it from time to time, or crossed it. The hundred feet it traversed seemed so much more when measured by the trail.

The two had come almost to the forest side of the jungle when a sharp turn in the path brought Thandar face to face with a huge bearlike man.

The fellow wore a g-string of soft hide, and over one shoulder dangled an old and filthy leopard skin — otherwise, he was naked. His thick, coarse hair was matted low over his forehead. The balance of his face was covered by a bushy red beard.

At sight of Thandar, his close-set little eyes burned with sullen rage and cunning. From his thick lips burst a savage yell — it was the preliminary challenge.

Ordinarily a certain amount of vituperation and coarse insults must pass between strangers meeting upon this inhospitable isle before they fly at one another's throat.

"I am Thurg," bellowed the brute. "I can kill you," and then followed a volley of vulgar allusions to Thandar's possible origin and the origin of his ancestors.

"The bad men," whispered Nadara.

With her words there swept into the man's memory the scene upon the face of the cliff that night a year before when, even in the throes of cowardly terror, he had turned to do battle with a huge caveman that the fellow might not prevent the escape of Nadara.

He glanced at the right forearm of the creature who faced him. A smile touched Thandar's lips — the arm was crooked as from the knitting of a broken bone, poorly set.

"You would kill Thandar — again?" he asked tauntingly, pointing toward the deformed member.

Then came recognition to the red-rimmed eyes of Thurg, as, with another ferocious bellow, he launched himself toward the author of his old hurt.

Thandar met the charge with his short stick of pointed hardwood — his "sword" he called it. It entered the fleshy part of Thurg's breast, calling forth a howl of pain and a trickling stream of crimson.

Thurg retreated. This was no way to fight. He was scandalized.

For several minutes he stood glaring at his foe, screaming hideous threats and insults at him. Then once more he charged.

Again the painful point entered his body, but this time he pressed in clutching madly at the goad and for a hold upon Thandar's body.

The latter held Thurg at arm's length, prodding him with the fire-hardened point of his wooden sword.

The caveman's little brain wondered at the skill and prowess of this stranger who had struck him a single blow with a cudgel many moons before and then run like a rabbit to escape his wrath.

Why was it that he did not run now? What strange change had taken place in him? He had expected an easy victim when he finally had recognized his foe; but instead he had met with brawn and ferocity equal to his own — and with a strange weapon, the like of which he had never before had seen.

Thandar was puncturing him rapidly now, and Thurg was screaming in rage and suffering. Presently he could endure it no longer. With a sudden wrench he tore himself loose and ran, bellowing, through the jungle.

Thandar did not pursue. It was enough that he had rid himself of his enemy. He turned toward Nadara, smiling.

"It will seem very tame in Boston," he said; but though she gave him an answering smile, she did not understand, for to her Boston was but another land of primeval forests, and dense jungles; of hairy, battling men, and fierce beasts.

At the edge of the forest they came again upon Thurg, but this time he was surrounded by a score of his burly tribesmen. Thandar knew better than to pit himself against so many.

Thurg came rushing down upon them, his fellows at his heels. In loud tones he screamed anew his challenge, and the beasts behind him took it up until the forest echoed to their hideous bellowing.

He had seen Nadara as he had battled with Thandar, and recognized her as the girl he had desired a year before — the girl whom this stranger had robbed him of.

Now he was determined to wreak vengeance on the man and at the same time recapture the girl.

Thandar and Nadara turned back into the jungle where but a single enemy could attack them at a time in the narrow trails. Here they managed to elude pursuit for several hours, coming again into the forest nearly a mile below the beach where the *Priscilla* had lain at anchor.

Thurg and his fellows had apparently given up the chase — they had neither seen nor heard aught of them for some time. Now the two hastened back through the wood to reach a point on the shore opposite the yacht.

At last they came in sight of the harbor. Thandar halted. A look of horror and disappointment supplanted the expression of pleasurable anticipation that had lighted his countenance — the yacht was not there.

A mile out they discerned her, steaming rapidly north.

Thandar ran to the beach. He tore the black panther's hide from his shoulders, waving it frantically above his head, the while he shouted in futile endeavor to attract attention from the dwindling craft.

Then, quite suddenly, he collapsed upon the beach, burying his face in his hands.

Presently Nadara crept close to his side. Her soft arms encircled his shoulders as she drew his cheek close to hers in an attempt to comfort him.

"Is it so terrible," she asked, "to be left here alone with your Nadara?"

"It is not that," he answered. "If you were mine I should not care so much, but you cannot be mine until we have reached civilization and you have been made mine in accordance wit the laws and customs of civilized men. And now who knows when another ship may come — if ever another will come?"

"But I am yours, Thandar," insisted the girl. "You are my man — you have told me that you love me, and I have replied that I would be your mate — who can give us to each other better than we can give ourselves?"

He tried, as best he could, to explain to her the marriage customs and ceremonies of his own world, but she found it difficult to understand how it might be that a stranger whom neither might possibly ever have seen before could make it right for her to love her Thandar, or that it would be wrong for her to love him without the stranger's permission.

To Thandar the future looked most black and hopeless. With his sudden determination to take Nadara back to his own people he had been overwhelmed with a mad yearning for home.

He realized that his past apathy to the idea of returning to Boston had been due solely to recollection of Boston as he had known it — Boston without Nadara; but now that she was to have gone back with him Boston seemed the most desirable spot in the world.

As he sat pondering the unfortunate happenings that had so delayed them that the yacht had sailed before they reached the shore, he also cast about for some plan to mitigate their disappointment.

To live forever on this savage island did not seem such an appalling thing as it had a year before — but then he had not realized his love for the wild young creature at his side. Ah, if she could but be made his wife, then his exile here would be a happy rather than a doleful lot.

What if he had been born here too? With the thought came a new idea that seemed to offer an avenue from his dilemma. Had he, too, been native born how would he have wed Nadara?

Why through the ceremony of their own people, of course. And if men and women were thus wed here, living together in faithfulness throughout their lives, what more sacred a union could civilization offer?

He sprang to his feet.

"Come, Nadara!" he cried. "We shall return to your people, and there you shall become my wife."

Nadara was puzzled, but she made no comment; content simply to leave the future to her lord and master; to do whatever would bring Thandar the greatest happiness.

The return to the dwellings of Nadara's people occupied three never-to-be-forgotten days.

How different this journey by comparison with that of a year since, when the cave girl had been leading the terror-stricken Waldo Emerson in flight from the bad men toward, to him, an equally horrible fate at the hands of Korth and Flatfoot!

Then the forest glades echoed to the pads of fierce beasts and the stealthy passage of naked, human horrors. No twig snapped that did not portend instant and terrifying death.

Now Korth and Flatfoot were dead at the hands of the metamorphosed Waldo. The racking cough was gone. He had encountered the bad men and others like them and come away with honors. Even Nagoola, the sleek, black devil-cat of the hideous nights, no longer sent the slightest tremor though the rehabilitated nerves.

Did not Thandar wear Nagoola's pelt about his shoulder and loins — a pelt that he had taken in hand-to-hand encounter with the dread beast?

Slowly they walked beneath the shade of giant trees, beside pleasant streams, or, again, across open valleys were the grass grew knee-high and countless, perfumed wild flowers opened a pathway before their naked feet.

At night they slept where night found them. Sometimes in the deserted lair of a wild beast, or again perched among the branches of a spreading tree where parallel branches permitted the construction of rude platforms.

And Thandar was always most solicitous to see that Nadara's couch was of the softest grasses and that his own lay at a little distance from hers and in a position where he might best protect her from prowling beasts.

Again was Nadara puzzled, but still she made no comment.

Finally they came to her village.

Several of the younger men came forth to meet them; but when they saw that the man was he who had slain Korth they bridled their truculence, all but one, Big Fist, who had assumed the role of king since Flatfoot had left.

"I can kill you," he announced by way of greeting, "for I am Big Fist, and until Flatfoot returns I am king — and maybe afterward, for some day I shall kill Flatfoot."

"I do not wish to fight you," replied Thandar. "Already have I killed Korth, and Flatfoot will return no more, for Flatfoot I have killed also. And I can kill Big Fist, but what is the use? Why should we fight? Let us be friends, for we must live together, and if we do not kill one another there will be more of us to meet the bad men, should they come, and kill them."

When Big Fist heard that Flatfoot was dead and by the hand of this stranger he pined less to measure his strength with that of the newcomer. He saw the knothole that the other offered, and promptly he sought to crawl through it, but with honor.

"Very well," he said, "I shall not kill you – you need not be afraid. But you must know that I am king, and do as I say that you shall do."

"'Afraid,'" Thandar laughed. "You may be king," he said, "but as for doing what you say –" and again he laughed.

It was a very different Waldo Emerson Smith-Jones from the thing that the sea had spewed up twelve months before.

II

KING THANDAR

*T*he first thing that Thandar did after he entered the village was to seek out Nadara's father.

They found the old man in the poorest and least protected cave in the cliff side, exposed to the attack of the first prowling carnivore, or skulking foeman.

He was sick, and there was none to care for him; but he did not complain. That was the way of his people. When a man became too old to be of service to the community it were better that he died, and so they did nothing to delay the inevitable. When one became an absolute burden upon his fellows it was customary to hasten the end – a carefully delivered blow with a heavy rock was calculated quickly to relieve the burdens of the community and the suffering of the invalid.

Thandar and Nadara came in and sat down beside him. The old fellow seemed glad to see them.

"I am Thandar," said the young man. "I wish to take your daughter as my mate."

The old man looked at him questioningly for a moment.

"You have killed Korth and Flatfoot — who is to prevent you from taking Nadara?"

"I wish to be joined to her with your permission an in accordance with the marriage ceremonies of your people," said Thandar.

The old man shook his head.

"I do not understand you," he replied at last. "There are several fine caves that are not occupied — if you wish a better one you have but to slay the present occupants if they do not get out when you tell them to — but I think they will get out when the slayer of Korth and Flatfoot tells them to."

"I am not worried about a cave," said Thandar. "Tell me how men take their wives among you."

"If they do not come with us willingly we take them by the hair and drag them with us," replied Nadara's father. "My mate would not come with me," he continued, "and even after I had caught her and dragged her to my cave she broke away and fled from me, but again I overhauled her, for when I was young none could run more swiftly, and this time I did what I should have done at first — I beat her upon the head until she went to sleep. When she awoke she was in my own cave, and it was night, and she did not try to run away anymore."

For a long time Thandar sat in thought. Presently he spoke addressing Nadara.

"In my country we do not take our wives in any such way, nor shall I take you thus. We must be married properly, according to the customs and laws of civilization."

Nadara made no reply. To her it seemed that Thandar must care very little for her — that was bout the only explanation she could put upon his strange behavior. It made her sad. And then the other women would laugh at her — of that she was quite certain, and that, too, made her feel very badly — they would see that Thandar did not want her.

The old man, lying upon his scant bed of matted, filthy grasses, had heard the conversation. He was as much at sea as Nadara. At last he spoke — very feebly now, for rapidly he was nearing dissolution.

"I am a very old man," he said to Thandar. "I have not long to live. Before I did I should like to know that Nadara has a mate who will protect her. I love her, though —" He hesitated.

"Though what?" asked Thandar.

"I have never told," whispered the old fellow. "My mate would not let me, but now that I am about to die it can do no harm. Nadara is not my daughter."

The girl sprang to her feet.

"Not your daughter? Then who am I?"

"I do not know who you are, except that you are not even of my people. All I know I will tell you now before I die. Come close, for my voice is dying faster than my body."

The young man and the girl came nearer to his side, and squatting there leaned close that they might catch each faintly articulated syllable.

"My mate and I," commenced the old man, "were childless, though many moons had passed since I took her to my cave. She wanted a little one, for thus only may women have aught upon which to lavish their love.

"We had been hunting together for several days alone and far from the village, for I was a great hunter when I was young — no greater ever lived among our people.

"And one day we came down to the great water, and there, a short distance from the shore, we saw a strange thing that floated upon the surface of the water, and when it was blown closer to us we saw that it was hollow and that in it were two people — a man and a woman. Both appeared to be dead.

"Finally I waded out to meet the thing, dragging it to shore, and there sure enough was a man and a woman, and the man was dead — quite dead. He must have been dead for a long time; but the woman was not dead.

"She was very fair, though her eyes and hair were black. We carried her ashore, and that night a little girl was born to her, but the woman died before morning.

"We put her back into the strange thing that had brought her — she and the dead man who had come with her — and shoved them off upon the great water, where the breeze, which runs away from the land twice each day, carried them out of sight, nor ever did we see them again.

"But before she sent them off my mate took from the body of the woman her strange coverings and a little bag of skin which contained many sparkling stones of different colors and metals of yellow and white made into things the purposes of which we could not guess.

"It was evident that the woman had come from a strange land, for she and all her belongings were unlike anything that either of us had ever seen before. She herself was different as Nadara is different — Nadara looks as her mother looked, for Nadara is the little babe that was born that night.

"We brought her back to our people after another moon, saying that she was born to my mate; but there was one woman who knew better, for it seemed that she had seen us when we found the boat, having been running away from a man who wanted her as his mate.

"But my mate did not want anyone to say that Nadara was not hers, for it is a great disgrace, as you well know, for a woman to be barren, and so she several times nearly killed this woman, who knew the truth, to keep her from telling it to the whole village.

"But I love Nadara as well as though she had been my own, and so I should like to see her well mated before I die."

Thandar had gone white during the narration of the story of Nadara's birth. He could scarce restrain an impulse to go upon his knees and thank his God that he had harked to the call of his civilized training rather than have given in to the easier way, the way these primitive, beastlike people offered. Providence, he thought, must indeed have sent him here to rescue her.

The old man, turning upon his rough pallet, fastened his sunken eyes questioningly upon Thandar. Nadara, too, with parted lips waited for him to speak. The old man gasped for breath — there was a strange rattling sound in his throat.

Thandar leaned above him, raising his head and shoulders slightly. The young man never had heard that sound before, but now that he heard it he needed no interpreter.

The locust, rubbing his legs along his wings, startles the uninitiated into the belief that a hidden rattler lurks in the pathway; but when the great diamond back breaks forth in warning none mistakes him for a locust.

And so it is with the death rattle in the human throat.

Thandar knew that it was the end. He saw the old man's mighty effort to push back the grim reaper that he might speak once more. In the dying eyes were a question and a plea. Thandar could not misunderstand.

He reached forward and took Nadara's hand.

"In my own land we shall be mated," he said. "None other shall wed with Nadara, and as proof that she is Thandar's she shall wear this always," and from his finger he slipped a splendid solitaire to the third finger of Nadara's left hand.

The old man saw. A look of relief and contentment that was almost a smile settled upon his features, as, with a gasping sigh, he sank limply into Thandar's arms, dead.

That afternoon several of the younger men carried the body of Nadara's foster father to the top of the cliff, depositing it about half a mile from the caves. There was no ceremony. In it, though, Waldo Emerson saw what might have been the first human funeral cortege — simple, sensible and utilitarian — from which the human race has retrograded to the ostentatious, ridiculous, pestilent burials of present day civilization.

The young men, acting under Big Fist's orders, carried the worthless husk to a safe distance from the caves, leaving it there to the rapid disintegration provided by the beasts and birds of prey.

Nadara wept, silently. An elderly lady with a single tooth espying her, moaned in sympathy. Presently other females, attracted by the moaning, joined them, and, becoming affected by the strange hysteria to which womankind is heir, mingled their moans with those of the toothless one.

Excited by their own noise they soon were shrieking and screaming in hideous chorus. Then came Big Fist and others of the men. The din annoyed them. They set upon the mourners with their fists and teeth scattering them in all directions. This ended the festivities.

Or would have had not Big Fist made the fatal mistake of launching a blow on Nadara. Thandar had been standing nearby looking with wonder upon the strange scene.

He had noted the quiet grief of the young girl — real grief; and he had witnessed the hysterical variety of the "mourners" — no sham grief. Precisely, because they made no pretense to grief — it was noise to which they aspired. And as the fiendish din had set his own nerves on edge he wondered not at all that Big Fist and the other men should take steps to quell the tumult.

The female half-brutes were theirs and Waldo Emerson had reverted sufficiently to the primitive to feel no incentive to interfere. But Nadara was not theirs — she was not of them and even had she not belonged to him the American would have felt bound to stand between her and the savage creatures among whom fate had cast her.

That she did belong to him, however, sent him hot with the blood lust of the killer as he sprang to intercept the rush of Big Fist toward her.

Waldo Emerson Smith-Jones had learned nothing of the manly art of self-defense in that other life that had been so zealously guarded from the rude and vulgar. This was unfortunate since it would have given him a great advantage over the man-brute. A single well-timed swing to that unguarded chin would have ended hostilities at once; but of hooks and jabs and jolts, scientific, Thandar knew nothing.

Except for his crude weapons he was as primeval in battle as his original anthropoid progenitor, and quite as often as not he forgot all about his sword, his knife, his bow and arrows and his spear when, half stooped, he crouched to meet the charge of a foeman.

Now he sprang for Big Fist's hairy throat. There was a sullen thud as the two bodies met, and then, rolling, biting and tearing, they struggled hither and thither upon the rocky ground at the base of the cliff.

The other men desisted from their attack upon the women. The women ceased their vocal mourning. In a little circled they formed about the contestants — a circle which moved this way and that as the fighters moved, keeping them always in the center.

Nadara forced her way through them to the front. She wished to be near Thandar. In her hand she carried a jagged bit of granite — one could never tell.

Big Fist was burly — mountainous — but Thandar was muscled like Nagoola, the black panther. His movements were all grace and each, but oh, so irresistible. A sudden and unexpected blow upon the side of Big Fist's head bent that bullet-shaped thing sideward with a jerk that almost dislocated the neck.

Big Fist shrieked with the pain of it. Thandar, delighted by the result of the accidental blow, repeated it. Big Fist bellowed — agonized. He made a last supreme effort to close with his agile foeman, and succeeded. His teeth sought Thandar's throat, but the act brought his own jugular close to Thandar's jaws.

The strong white teeth of Waldo Emerson Smith-Jones closed upon it as naturally as though no countless ages had rolled their snaillike way between himself and the last of his progenitors to bury bloody fangs in the soft flesh of an antagonist.

Wasted ages! Fleeing from the primitive and the brute toward the neoteric and the human — in a brief instant your labors are undone, the veneer of eons crumbles in the heat of some pristine passion revealing again naked and unashamed the primitive and the brute.

Big Fist, white now from terror at impending death, struggled to be free. Thandar buried his teeth more deeply. There was a sudden rush of spurting blood that choked him. Big Fist relaxed, inert.

Thandar, drenched crimson, rose to his feet. The huge body on the ground before him floundered spasmodically once or twice as the life blood rushed from the severed jugular. The eyes rolled up and set, there was a final twitch and Big Fist was dead.

Thandar turned toward the circle of interested spectators. He singled out a burly quartet.

"Bear Big Fist to the cliff top," he commanded. "When you return we shall chose a new king."

The men did as they were bid. They did not at all understand what Thandar meant about choosing a king. Having slain Big Fist, Thandar was king, unless some ambitious one desired to dispute his right to reign. But all had seen him slay Big Fist, and all knew that he had killed Korth and Flatfoot, so who was there would dare question his kingship?

When they had come back to the village Thandar gathered them beneath a great tree that grew close to the base of the cliff. Here they squatted upon their haunches in a rough circle. Behind them stood the women and children, wide-eyed and curious.

"Let us chose a king," said Thandar, when all had come.

There was a long silence, then one of the older men spoke.

"I am an old man. I have seen many kings. They come by killing. They go by killing. Thandar has killed two kings. Now he is king. Who wishes to kill Thandar and become king?"

There was no answer.

The old man arose.

"It was foolish to come here to choose a king," he said, "when a king we already have."

"Wait," commanded Thandar. "Let us chose a king properly. Because I have killed Flatfoot and Big Fist does not prove that I can make a good king. Was Flatfoot a good king?"

"He was a bad man," replied the ancient one.

"Has a good man ever been king?" asked Thandar.

The old fellow puckered his brow in thought.

"Not for a long time."

"That is because you always permit a bully and a brute to rule you," said Thandar. "That is not the proper way to choose a king. Rather you should come together as we are come, and among you talk over the needs of the tribe and when you are decided as to what measures are best for the welfare of the members of the tribe then should you select the man best fitted to carry out your plans. That is a better way to choose a king."

The old man laughed.

"And then," he said, "would come a Big Fist or a Flatfoot and slay our king that he might be king in his place."

"Have you ever seen a man who could slay all the other men of the tribe at the same time?"

The old man looked puzzled.

"That is my answer to your argument," said Thandar. "Those who choose the king can protect him from his enemies. So long as he is a good king they should do so, but when he becomes a bad king they can then select another, and if the bad king refuses to obey the new it would be an easy matter for several men to kill him or drive him away, no matter how mighty a fighter he might be."

Several of the men nodded understandingly.

"We had not thought of that," they said. "Thandar is indeed wise."

"So now," continued the American, "let us choose a king whom the majority of us want, and then so long as he is a good king the majority of us must fight for him and protect him. Let us choose a man whom we know to be a good man regardless of his ability to kill his fellows, for if he has the majority of the tribe to fight for him what need will he have to fight for himself? What we want is a wise man — one who can lead the tribe to fertile lands and good hunting, and in the time of battle direct the fighting intelligently. Flatfoot and Big Fist had not brains enough between them to do aught but steal the mates of other men. Such should not be the business of kings. Your king should protect your mates from such as Flatfoot, and he should punish those who would steal them."

"But how may he do these things?" asked a young man, "if he is not the best fighter in the tribe?"

"Have I not shown you how?" asked Thandar. "We who make him king shall be his fighters — he will not need to fight with his own hands."

Again there was a long silence. Then the old man spoke again.

"There is wisdom in the talk of Thandar. Let us choose a king who will have to be good to us if he wishes to remain king. It is very bad for us to have a king whom we fear."

"I, for one," said the young man who had previously spoken, "do not care to be ruled by a king unless he is able to defeat me in battle. If I can defeat him then I should be king."

And so they took sides, but at last they compromised by selecting one whom they knew to be wise and a great fighter as well. Thus they chose Thandar king.

"Once each week," said the new king, "we shall gather here and talk among ourselves of the things which are for the best good of the tribe, and what seems best to the majority shall be done. The tribe will tell the king what to do — the king will carry out the work. And all must fight when the king says fight and all must work when the king says work, for we shall all be fighting or working for the whole tribe, and I, Thandar, your king, shall fight and work the hardest of you all."

It was a new idea to them and placed the kingship in a totally different light from any by which they had previously viewed it. That it would take a long time for them to really absorb the idea Thandar knew, and he was glad that in the meantime they had a king who could command their respect according to their former standards.

And he smiled when he thought of the change that had taken place in him since first he had sat trembling, weeping, and coughing upon the lonely shore before the terrifying forest.

III

THE GREAT NAGOOLA

*W*aldo Emerson Smith-Jones had gladly embraced the opportunity which chance had offered him to assume the kingship of the little tribe of troglodytes. First, because his position would assure Nadara greater safety, and, second, because of the opening it would give him for the exercise of his new-found initiative.

Where before he had shrunk from responsibility he now found himself anxious to assume it. He longed to do, where formerly he had been content to but read of the accomplishments of others.

To his chagrin, however, he soon discovered that the classical education to which his earlier life had been devoted under the guidance of a fond and ultra-cultured mother was to prove a most inadequate foundation upon which to build a practical scheme of life for himself and his people.

He wished to teach his tribe to construct permanent and comfortable houses, but he could not recollect any practical hints on carpentry that he had obtained from Ovid.

His people lived by hunting small rodents, robbing birds' nets, and gathering wild fruit and vegetables. Thandar desired to institute a scheme of community farming, but the works of the Cyclic Poets, with which he was quite familiar, seemed to offer little of value along agricultural lines. He regretted that he had not matriculated at an agricultural college west of the Alleghenies rather than at Harvard.

However, he determined to do the best he could with the meager knowledge he possessed of things practical — a knowledge so meager that it consisted almost entirely of the bare definition of the word agriculture.

It was a germ, however, for it presupposed a knowledge of the results that might be obtained through agriculture.

So Thandar found himself a step ahead of the earliest of his progenitors who had through to plant purposely the seeds that nature heretofore had distributed haphazard through the agencies of wind and bird and beast; but only a step ahead.

He realized that he occupied a very remarkable position in the march of ages. He had known and seen and benefited by all the accumulated knowledge of ages of progression from the stone age to the twentieth century, and now, suddenly, fate had snatched him back into the stone age, or possibly a few æons farther back, only to show him that all that he had from a knowledge of other men's knowledge was keen dissatisfaction with the stone age.

He had lived in houses of wood and brick and looked through windows of glass. He had read in the light of gas and electricity, and he even knew of candles; but he could not fashion the tools to build a house, he could not have made a brick to have saved his life, glass had suddenly become one of the wonders of the world to him, and as for gas and electricity and candles they had become one with the mystery of the Sphinx.

He could write verse in excellent Greek, but he was no longer proud of that fact. He would much rather that he had been able to tan a hide, or make fire without matches. Waldo Emerson Smith-Jones had a year ago been exceedingly proud of his intellect and his learning, but for a year his ego had been shrinking until now he felt himself the most pitiful ignoramus on earth. "Criminally ignorant," he said to Nadara, "for I have thrown away the opportunities of a lifetime devoted to the accumulation of useless erudition when I might have been profiting by the practical knowledge which has dragged the world from the black pit of barbarism to the light of modern achievement — I might not only have done this but, myself, added something to the glory and welfare of mankind. I am no good, Nadara — worse than useless."

The girl touched his strong brown hand caressingly, looking proudly into his eyes.

"To me you are very wonderful, Thandar," she said. "With your own hands you slew Nagoola, the most terrible beast in the world, and Korth, and Flatfoot, and Big Fist lie dead beneath the vultures because of your might — single-handed you killed them all; three awesome men. No, my Thandar is greater than all other men."

Nor could Waldo Emerson repress the swelling tide of pride that surged through him as the girl he loved recounted his exploits. No longer did he think of his achievements as "vulgar physical prowess." The old Waldo Emerson, whose temperature had risen regularly at three o'clock each afternoon, whose pitifully skinny body had been racked by coughing continually, whose eyes had been terror filled by day and night at the rustling of dry leaves, was dead.

In his place stood a great, full-blooded man, brown skinned and steel thewed; fearless, self-reliant, almost brutal in his pride of power — Thandar, the caveman.

The months that passed as Thandar led his people from one honeycombed cliff to another as he sought a fitting place for a permanent village were filled with happiness for Nadara and the king.

The girl's happiness was slightly alloyed by the fact that Thandar failed to claim her as his own. She could not yet quite understand the ethics which separated them. Thandar tried repeatedly to explain to her that some day they were to return to his own world, and that that world would not accept her unless she had been joined to him according to the rites and ceremonies which it had originated.

"Will this marriage ceremony of which you tell me make you love me more?" asked Nadara.

Thandar laughed and took her in his arms.

"I could not love you more," he replied.

"Then of what good is it?"

Thandar shook his head.

"It is difficult to explain," he said, "especially to such a lovable little pagan as my Nadara. You must be satisfied to know — accept my word for it — that it is because I love you that we must wait."

Now it was the girl's turn to shake her head.

"I cannot understand," she said. "My people take their mates as they will and they are satisfied and everybody is satisfied and all is well; but their king, who may mate as he chooses, waits until a man whom he does not know and who lives across the great water where we may never go, gives him permission to mate with one who loves him — with one whom he *says* he loves."

Thandar noticed the emphasis which Nadara put upon the word "says."

"Some day," he said, "when we have reached my world you will know that I was right, and you will thank me. Until then, Nadara, you must trust me, and," he added half to himself, "God knows I have earned your trust even if you do not know it."

And so Nadara made believe that she was satisfied but in her heart of hearts she still feared that Thandar did not really love her, nor did the half-veiled comments of the women add at all to her peace of mind.

During all the time that Thandar was with her he had been teaching her his language for he had set his heart upon taking her home, and he wished her to be as well prepared for her introduction to Boston and civilization as he could make her.

Thandar's plan was to find a suitable location within sight of the sea that he might always be upon the lookout for a ship. At last he found such a place — a level meadow land upon a low plateau overlooking the ocean.

He had come upon it while he wandered alone several miles from the temporary cliff dwellings the tribe was occupying. The soil, when he dug into it, he found to be rich and black. There was timber upon once side and upon the other over-hanging cliffs of soft limestone.

It was Thandar's plan to build a village partly of logs against the face of the cliff, burrowing inward behind the dwellings for such additional apartments as each family might require.

The caves alone would have proved sufficient shelter, but the man hoped by compelling his people to construct a portion of each dwelling of logs to engender within each family a certain feeling of ownership and pride in personal possession as would make it less easy for them to give up their abodes than in the past, when it had been necessary but to move to another cliff to find caves equally as comfortable as those which they had so easily abandoned.

In other words he hoped to give them a word which their vocabulary had never held — home.

Whether or not he would have succeeded we may never know, for fate stepped in at the last moment to alter with a single stroke his every plan and aspiration.

As he returned to his people that afternoon filled with the enthusiasm of his hopes a burly, hairy figure crept warily close to him. As Thandar emerged from the brush which reaches close to the cliffs where the temporary encampment had been made Nadara, watching for him, ran forward to meet him.

The creature upon Thandar's trail halted at the edge of the bush. As the close-set eyes fell upon the girl his flabby lips vibrated to the quick intaking of his breath and his red lids half closed in cunning and desire.

For a few moments he watched the man and the maid as they turned and walked slowly toward the cliffs, the arm of the former about the brown shoulders of the latter. Then he too turned and melted into the tangled branches behind him.

That evening Thandar gathered the members of the tribe about him at the foot of the cliff. They sat around a great fire while Thandar, their king, explained to them in minutest detail the future that he had mapped out for them.

Some of the old men shook their heads, for here was an unheard of thing — a change from the accustomed ordering of their lives — and they were loath to change regardless of the benefits which might accrue.

But for the most part the people welcomed the idea of comfortable and permanent habitations, though their antici-patory joy, Thandar reasoned, was due largely to a childish eagerness for something new and different — whether their enthusiasm would survive the additional labors which the new life was sure to entail was another question.

So Thandar laid down the new laws that were to guide his people thereafter. The men were to make all implements and weapons, for he had already taught them to use arrows and spears. The women were to keep all edged tools sharp. The men were to hew the logs and build the houses — the women make garments, cook and keep the houses in order.

The men were to turn up the soil, the women were to sow the seeds, and cultivate the growing crops, which later, all hands must turn to and harvest.

The hunting and fighting devolved upon the men, but the fighting must be confined to enemies of the tribe. A man who killed another member of the tribe except in defense of his home or his own person was to suffer death.

Other laws he made — good laws — which even these primitive people could see where good. It was quite late when the last of them crawled into his comfortless cave to dream of large airy rooms built of the trees of the forest; of good food in plenty just before the rains as well as after; of security from the periodic raids of the "bad men."

Thandar and Nadara were the last to go. Together they sat upon a narrow ledge before Nadara's cave, the moonlight falling upon their glistening, naked shoulders, while they talked and dreamed together of the future.

Thandar had been talking of the wonderful plans which seemed to fill his whole mind — of the future of the tribe — of the great strides toward civilization they could make in a few brief years if they could but be made to follow the simple plans he had in mind.

"Why," he said, "in ten years they should have bridged a gulf that it must have required ages for our ancestors to span."

"And you are planning ten years ahead, Thandar," she asked, "when only yesterday you were saying that once beside the sea you hoped it would be but a short time before we might sight a passing vessel that would bear us away to your civilization? Must we wait ten years, Thandar?"

"I am planning for them," he replied. "We may not be here to witness the changes; but I wish to start them upon the road and when we go I shall see to it that a king is chosen in my place who has the courage and the desire to carry out my plans.

"Yet," he added, musingly, "it would be splendid could we but return to complete our work. Never, Nadara, have I performed a single constructive act for the benefit of my fellow man, but now I see an opportunity to do something, however small it may see, to — what was that?"

A low rumbling muttered threateningly out of the west. Deep and ominous it sounded, yet so low that it failed to awaken any member of the sleeping tribe.

Before either could again speak there came a slight trembling of the earth beneath them, scarcely sufficient to have been noticeable had it not been preceded by the distant grumbling in the earth's bowels.

The two upon the moonlit ledge came to their feet, and Nadara drew close to Thandar, the man's arm encircling her shoulders protectingly.

"The Great Nagoola," she whispered. "Again he seeks to escape."

"What do you mean?" asked Thandar. "It is an earthquake — distant and quite harmless to us."

"No, it is The Great Nagoola," insisted Nadara. "Long time ago, when our fathers' fathers were yet unborn, The Great Nagoola roamed the land devouring all that chanced to come in his way — men, beasts, birds, everything.

"One day my people came upon his sleeping in a deep gorge between two mountains. They were mighty men in those days, and when they saw their great enemy asleep there in the gorge half of them went upon one side and half upon the other, and they pushed the two mountains over into the gorge upon the sleeping beast, imprisoning him there.

"It is all true, for my mother had it from her mother, who in turn was told it by her mother — thus has it been handed down truthfully since it happened long time ago.

"And even in this day is occasionally heard the growling of The Great Nagoola in his anger, and the earth shakes a trembles as he strives, far, far beneath to shake the mountains from him and escape. Did you not hear his voice and feel the ground rock?"

Thandar laughed.

"Well, we're quite safe then," he cried, "for with two mountains piled upon him he cannot escape."

"Who knows?" asked Nadara. "He is huge — as huge, himself, as a small mountain. Some day, they say, he will escape, and then naught will pacify his rage until he has destroyed every living creature upon the land."

"Do not worry, little one," said Thandar. "The Great Nagoola will have to grumble louder and struggle more fiercely before ever he may dislodge the two mountains. Even now he is quiet again, so run to your cave, sweetheart, nor bother your pretty head with useless worries — it is time that all good people were asleep," and he stooped and kissed her as she turned to go.

For a moment she clung to him.

"I am afraid, Thandar," she whispered. "Why, I do not know. I only know that I am afraid, with a great fear that will not be quiet."

IV

THE BATTLE

*E*arly the following morning while several of the women and children were at the river drawing water the balance of the tribe of Thandar was startled into wakefulness by piercing shrieks from the direction the water carriers had taken.

Before the great, hairy men, led by the smooth-skinned Thandar, had reached the foot of the cliff in their rush to the rescue of the women several of the latter appeared at the edge of the forest, running swiftly toward the caves.

Mingled with their screams of terror were cries of, "The bad men! The bad men!" But these were not needed to acquaint the rescuers with the cause of the commotion, for at the heels of the women came Thurg and a score of his vicious brutes. Little better than anthropoid apes were they. Long armed, hairy, skulking monsters, whose close-set eyes and retreating foreheads proclaimed more intimate propinquity to the higher orders of brutes than to civilized man.

Woe betide male or female who fell into their remorseless clutches, since to the base passions, unrestrained, that mark the primordial they were addicted to the foulest forms of cannibalism.

In the past their raids upon their neighbors for meat and women had met with but slight resistance — the terrified cave dwellers scampering to the safety of their dizzy ledges from which they might hurl stones and roll boulders down to the confusion of any foe however ferocious.

Always the bad men caught a few unwary victims before the safety of the ledges could be attained, but this time there was a difference. Thurg was delighted. The men were rushing downward to meet him — great indeed would be the feast which should follow this day's fighting, for with the men disposed of there would be but little difficulty in storming the cliff and carrying off all the women and children, and as he though upon these things there floated in his little brain the image of the beautiful girl he had watched come down the evening before from the caves to meet the smooth-skinned warrior who trice now had bested Thurg in battle.

That Thandar's men might turn the tables upon him never for a moment occurred to Thurg. Nor was there little wonder, since, mighty as were the muscles of the cave men, they were weaklings by comparison with the half-brutes of Thurg — only the smooth-skinned stranger troubled the muddy mind of the near-man.

It puzzled him a little, though, to see the long slim sticks that the enemy carried, and the little slivers of in skin bags upon their backs, and the strange curved branches whose ends were connected by slender bits of gut. What were these things for?

Soon he was to know — this and other things.

Thandar's warriors did not rush upon Thurg and his brutes in a close packed, yelling mob. Instead they trotted slowly forward in a long thin line that stretched out parallel with the base of the cliff. In the center, directly in front of the charging bad men, was Thandar, calling directions to his people, first upon one hand and then upon the other.

And in accordance with his commands the ends of the line began to quicken the pace, so that quickly Thurg saw that there were men before him, and men upon either hand, and now, at fifty feet, while all were advancing cautiously, crouched for the final hand-to-hand encounter, he saw the enemy slip each sliver into the gut of the bent branches — there was a sudden chorus of twangs and Thurg felt a sharp pain in his neck. Involuntarily he clapped his hand to the spot to find one of the slivers sticking there, scarcely an inch from his jugular.

With a howl of rage he snatched the thing from him, and as he leaped to charge to punish these audacious madmen he noted a dozen of his henchmen plucking silvers from various portions of their bodies, while two lay quite still upon the grass with just the end of slivers protruding from their breasts.

The sight brought the beast-man to a momentary halt. He saw his fellows charging in upon the foe — he saw another volley of slivers speed from the bent branches. Down went another of his fighters, and then the enemy cast aside their strange weapons at a shouted command from the smooth-skinned one and grasping their long, slim stick ran forward to meet Thurg's people.

Thurg smiled. It would soon be over now. He turned toward one who was bearing down upon him — it was Thandar. Thurg crouched to meet the charge. Rage, revenge, the lust for blood fired his bestial brain. With his huge paws he would tear the puny stick from this creature's grasp, and this time he would gain his hold upon that smooth throat. He licked his lips. And then out of the corner of his eyes he glanced to the right.

What strange sight was this! His people flying? It was incredible! And yet it was true. Growling and raging in pain and anger they were running a gauntlet of fire-sharpened lances. Three lay dead. The others were streaming blood as they fled before the relentless prodding devils at their backs.

It was enough for Thurg. He did not wait to close with Thandar. A single howl of dismay broke from his flabby lips, and then he wheeled and dashed for the wood. He was the last to pass through the rapidly converging ends of Thandar's primitive battle line. He was running so fast that, afterward, Nadara who was watching the battle from the cliff-side insisted that his feet flew higher than his head at each frantic leap.

Thandar and his victorious army pursued the enemy through the wood for a mile or more, then they returned laughing and shouting, to receive the plaudits of the old men, the women, and the children.

It was a happy day. There was feasting. And Thandar, having in mind things he had read of savage races, improvised a dance in honor of the victory.

He knew little more of savage dances than his tribesmen did of the two-step and the waltz; but he knew that dancing and song and play marked in themselves a great step upward in the evolution of man from the lower orders, and so he meant to teach these things to his people.

A red flush spread to his temples as he thought of his dignified father and his stately mother and with what horrified emotions they would view him now could they but see him — naked but for a g-string and a panther skin, moving with leaps and bounds, and not stately waltz steps in a great circle, clapping his hands in time to his movements, while behind him strung a score of lusty, naked warriors, mimicking his every antic with the fidelity of apes.

About them squatted the balance of the tribe more intensely interested in this, the first ceremonial function of their lives, than with any other occurrence that had ever befallen them. They, too, now clapped their hands in time with the dancers.

Nadara stood with parted lips and wide eyes watching the strange scene. Within her it seemed that something was struggling for expression — something that she must have known long, long ago — something that she had forgotten but that she presently must recall. With it came an insistent urge — her feet could scarce remain quietly upon the ground, and great waves of melody and song welled into her heart and throat, though what they were and what they meant she did not know.

She only knew that she was intensely excited and happy and that her whole being seemed as light and airy as the soft wind that blew across the swaying treetops of the forest.

Now the dance was done. Thandar had led the warriors back to the feast. In the center of the circle where the naked bodies of the men had leaped and swirled to the clapping of many hands was an open space, deserted. Into it Nadara ran, drawn by some subtle excitement of the soul which she could not have fathomed had she tried — which she did not try to fathom.

Around her slim, graceful figure was draped the glossy black pelt of Nagoola — another trophy of the prowess of her man. It half concealed but to accentuate the beauties of her form.

With eyes half-closed she took a half dozen graceful, tentative steps. Now the eyes of Thandar and several others were upon her, but she did not see them. Suddenly, with outthrown arms, she commenced to dance, bending her lithe body, swaying from side to side as she fell, with graceful abandon, into steps and poses that seemed as natural to her as repose.

About the little circle she wove her simple yet intricate way, and now every eye was upon her as every savage heart leaped in unison with her shapely feet, rising and falling in harmony with her lithe, brown limbs.

And of all the hearts that leaped, fastest leaped the heart of Thandar, for he saw in the poetry of motion of the untutored girl the proof of her birthright — the truth of all that he had guessed of her origin since her foster father had related the story of her birth upon his deathbed. None up a child of an age-old culture could posses this inherent talent. Any moment expected her lips to break forth in song, nor was he to be disappointed, for presently, as the circling cave folk commended to clap their palms in time to her steps, Nadara lifted her voice in clear and birdlike notes — a wordless pæan of love and life and happiness.

At last, exhausted, she paused, and as her eyes fell upon Thandar they broke into a merry laugh.

"The king is not the only one who can leap and play upon his feet," she cried.

Thandar came to the center of the circle and kneeling at her fee took one of her hands in his and kissed it.

"The king is only mortal and a man," he said. "It is no reproach that he cannot equal the divine grace of a goddess. You are very wonderful, my Nadara," he continued, "from loving you I am coming to worship you."

And within the deep and silent wood another was stirred with mighty emotions by the sight of the half-naked, graceful girl. It was Thurg, the bad man, who had sneaked back alone to the edge of the forest that he might seek and opportunity to be revenged upon Thandar and his people.

Half formed in his evil brain had been a certain plan, which the sight of Nadara, dancing in the firelight, had turned to concrete resolution.

With the dancing and the feasting over, the tribe of Thandar betook itself by ones and twos to the rocky caves that they expected so soon to desert for the more comfortable village which they were to build under the direction of their king, to the east, beside the great water.

At last all was still — the village slept. No sentry guarded their slumbers, for Thandar, steeped in book learning, must needs add to his stock of practical knowledge by bitter experience, and never yet had the cause arisen for a night guard about his village.

Having defeated Thurg and his people he thought that they would not return again, and certainly not by night for the people of this wild island roamed seldom by night, having too much respect for the teeth and talons of Nagoola to venture forth after darkness had settled upon the grim forests and lonely plains.

But a tempest of uncontrolled emotions surged through the hairy breast of Thurg. He forgot Nagoola. He thought only of revenge — revenge and the black haired beauty who had so many times eluded him.

And as he saw her dancing in the circle of hand-clapping tribesmen, in the light of the brushwood fire, his desire for her became a veritable frenzy.

He could scarce restrain himself from rushing single-handed among his foes and snatching the girl before their faces. However, caution came to his rescue, and so he waited,

albeit impatiently, until the last of the cave folk had retired
to his cavern.

He had seen into which Nadara had withdrawn — one that
lay far up the face of the steep cliff and directly above the
cave occupied by Thandar. The moon was overcast, the fire
at the foot of the cliff had died to glowing embers, all was
wrapped in darkness and in shadow. Far in the depths of the
wood Nagoola coughed and cried. The weird sound raised
the coarse hair at the nape of Thurg's bull neck. He cast an
apprehensive backward glance, then, crouching low, he
moved quickly and silently across the clearing toward the base
of the cliff.

Flattened against a protruding boulder, there he waited,
listening, for a moment. No sound broke the stillness of the
sleeping village. None had seen his approach — of that he was
convinced.

Carefully he began the ascent of the cliff face, made difficult by the removal of the rough ladders that led from ledge
to ledge by day, but which were withdrawn with the retiring
of the community to their dark holes.

But Thurg had dragged with him from the forest a slim
sapling. This he leaned against the face of the cliff. Its up-
tilted end just topped the lowest ledge.

Thurg was almost as large and quite as clumsy in appearance as a gorilla, yet he was not as far removed form his true
arboreal ancestors as is the great simian, and so he accom-
plished in silence and with evident ease what his great bulk
might have seemed to have relegated to the impossible.

Like a huge cat he scrambled up the frail pole until his
fingers clutched the ledge edge above him. Apelike he drew
himself to a squatting position there. Then he groped for the
ladder that the cave folk had drawn up from below.

This he erected to the next ledge above. Thereafter the way
was easy, for the balance of the ledges were connected by
steeply inclined trails cut into the cliff face. This had been an
innovation of Thandar's, who considered the rickety ladders
not only a nuisance, but extremely dangerous to life and limb,
for scarce a day passed that some child or woman did not
receive a bad fall because of them.

So Thurg, with Thandar's unintentional aid, came easily to the mouth of Nadara's cave.

Great had been the temptation as he passed the cave below to enter and slay his enemy. Never had Thurg so hated any creature as he hated this smooth-skinned interloper — with all the venom of his mean soul he hated him.

Now he stooped, listening, just inside the entrance of the cave. He could hear the regular breathing of the girl within. The hot blood surged through his brute veins. His huge paws opened and closed spasmodically. His breath sucked hot between his flabby lips.

Just beneath him Thandar lay dreaming. He saw a wonderful vision of a beautiful nymph dancing in the firelight. In a circle about her sat the Smith-Joneses, the Percy Standishes, the Livingston-Browns, the Quincy Adams-Cootses, and a hundred more equally aristocratic families of Boston.

It did not seem strange to Thandar that there was not enough clothing among the entire assemblage to have decently draped the Laocoön. His father wore a becoming loin cloth, while the stately Mrs. John Alden Smith-Jones, his mother, was tastefully arrayed in a scant robe of the skins of small rodents sewn together with bits of gut.

As the nymph danced the audience kept time to her steps with loudly clapping palms, and when she was done they approached her one by one, crawling upon their hands and knees, and kissed her hand.

Suddenly he saw that the nymph was Nadara, and as he sprang forward to claim her a large man with a coarse matted beard, a slanted forehead, and close-set eyes, leaped out from among the others, seized Nadara and fled with her toward a waiting trolley car.

He recognized the man as Thurg, and even in his dream it seemed rather incongruous that he could be clothed in well-fitting evening clothes.

Nadara screamed once, and the scream roused Thandar from his dream. Raising upon one elbow he looked toward the entrance of his cave. The recollection of the dream swept back into his memory. With a little sigh of relief that it had been but a dream, he settled back once more upon his bed of grasses, and soon was wrapped in dreamless slumber.

V

THE ABDUCTION OF NADARA

*C*autiously Thurg crawled into the cave where Nadara slept upon her couch of soft grasses, wrapped in the glossy pelt of Nagoola, the black panther.

The hulking form of the beast-man blotted out the faint light that filtered from the lesser darkness of the night without through the jagged entrance to the cave.

All within was in Stygian gloom.

Groping with his hands Thurg came at last upon a corner of the grassy pallet. Softly he wormed inch by inch closer to the sleeper. Now his fingers felt the thick fur of the panther skin.

Lightly, for so gross a thing, his touch followed the recumbent figure of the girl until his giant paws felt the silky luxuriance of her raven hair.

For an instant he paused. Then, quickly and silently, one great palm clapped roughly over Nadara's mouth, while the other arm encircled her waist, lifting her from her bed.

Awakened and terrified, Nadara struggled to free herself and to scream; but the giant hand across her mouth effectually sealed her lips, while the arm about her waist held her as firmly as might iron bands.

Thurg spoke no word, but as Nadara's hands came in contact with his hairy breast and matted beard as she fought for freedom she guessed the identity of her abductor, and shuddered.

Waiting only to assure himself that his hold upon his prisoner was secure and that no trailing end of her robe might trip him in his flight down the cliff face, Thurg commenced the descent.

Opposite the entrance to Thandar's cave Nadara redoubled her efforts to free her mouth that she might scream aloud but once. Thurg, guessing her desire, pressed his palm the tighter, and in a moment the two had passed unnoticed to the ledge below.

Down the winding trail of the upper ledges Thurg's task was comparatively easy — thanks to Thandar, but at the second ledge from the bottom of the cliff he was compelled to take to the upper of the two ladders which completed the way to the ground below.

And here it was necessary to remove his hand from Nadara's mouth. In a low growl he warned her to silence with threats of instant death, then he removed his hand from across her face, grasped the top of the ladder and swung over the dangerous height with his burden under his arm.

For an instant Nadara was too paralyzed with terror to take advantage of her opportunity, but just as Thurg set foot upon the ledge at the bottom of the ladder she screamed aloud once.

Instantly Thurg's hand fell roughly across her lips. Brutally he shook her, squeezing her body in his mighty grip until she gasped for breath, and each minute expected to feel her ribs snap to the terrific strain.

For a moment Thurg stood silently upon the ledge, compressing the tortured body of his victim and listening for signs of pursuit from above.

Presently the agony of her suffering overcame Nadara — she swooned. Thurg felt her form relax, and his flabby lips twisted to a hideous grin.

The cliff was quiet — the girl's scream had not disturbed the slumbers of her tribesmen. Thurg swung the ladder he had just descended over the edge of the cliff below, and a moment later he stood at the bottom with his burden.

Without noise he removed the ladder and the sapling that he had used in his ascent, laying them upon the ground at the foot of the cliff. This would halt, temporarily, any pursuit until the cave men could bring other ladders from the higher levels, where they doubtless had them hidden.

But no pursuit developed, and Thurg disappeared into the dark forest with his prize.

For a long distance he carried her, his little pig eyes searching and straining to right and left into the black night for the first sign of savage beast. The half atrophied muscles of his little ears, still responding to an almost dead instinct, strove to prick those misshapen members forward that they might catch the first crackling of dead leaves beneath the padded paw of the fanged night prowlers.

But the wood seemed dead. No living creature appeared to thwart the beast-man's evil intent. Far behind him Thandar slept. Thurg grinned.

The moon broke through the clouds, splotching the ground all silver-green beneath the forest trees. Nadara awoke from her swoon. They were in a little open glade. Instantly she recalled the happenings that had immediately preceded her unconsciousness. In the moonlight she recognized Thurg. He was smirking horribly down into her upturned face.

Thandar had often talked with her of religion. He had taught her of his God, and now the girl thanked Him that Thurg was still too low in the scale of evolution to have learned to kiss. To have had that matted beard, those flabby, pendulous lips pressed to hers! It was too horrible — she closed her eyes in disgust.

Thurg lowered her to her feet. With one hand he still clutched her shoulder. She saw him standing there before her — his greedy, blood-shot eyes devouring her. His awful lips shook and trembled as his hot breath sucked quickly in and out in excited gasps.

She knew that the end was coming. Frantically she cast about her for some means of defense or escape. Thurg was drawing her toward him.

Suddenly she drew back her clenched fist and struck him full in the mouth, then, tearing herself from his grasp, she turned and fled.

But in a moment he was upon her. Seizing her roughly by the shoulders he shook her viciously, hurling her to the ground.

The blood from his wounded lips dropped upon her face and throat.

From the distance came a deep toned, thunderous rumbling. Thurg raised his head and listened. Again and again came that awesome sound.

"The Great Nagoola is coming to punish you," whispered Nadara.

Thurg still remained squatting beside her. She had ceased to fight for now she felt that a greater power than hers was intervening to save her.

The ground beneath them trembled, shook and then tossed frightfully. The rumbling and the roaring became deafening. Thurg, his passion frozen in the face of this new terror, rose to his feet. For a moment there was a lull, then came another and more terrific shock.

The earth rose and fell sickeningly. Fissures opened, engulfing trees, and then closed like hungry mouths gulping food long denied.

Thurg was thrown to the ground. Now he was terror stricken. He screamed aloud in his fear.

Again there came a lull, and this time the beast-man leaped to his feet and dashed away into the forest. Nadara was alone.

Presently the earth commenced to tremble again, and the voice of The Great Nagoola rumbled across the world. Frightened animals scampered past Nadara, fleeing in all directions. Little deer, foxes, squirrels and other rodents in countless numbers scurried, terrified, about.

A great black panther and his mate trotted shoulder to shoulder into the glade where Nadara still stood too bewildered to know which way to fly.

They eyed her for a moment, as they paused in the moonlight, then without a second glance they loped away into the brush. Directly behind them came three deer.

Nadara realized that she had felt no fear of the panthers as she would have under ordinary circumstances. Even the little deer ran with their natural enemies. Every lesser fear was submerged in the overwhelming terror of the earthquake.

Dawn was breaking in the east. The rumblings were diminishing. The tremors at greater intervals and of lessening violence.

Nadara started to retrace her steps toward the village. Momentarily she looked to see Thandar coming in search of her, but she came to the edge of the forest and no sigh of Thandar or another of her tribesmen had come to cheer her.

At last she stepped into the open. Before her was the cliff. A cry of anguish broke from her lips at the sight that met her eyes. Torn, tortured and crumpled were the lofty crags that had been her home — the home of the tribe of Thandar.

The overhanging cliff top had broken away and lay piled in a jagged heap at the foot of the cliff. The caves had disappeared. The ledges had crumbled before the titanic struggles of The Great Nagoola. All was desolation and ruin.

She approached more closely. Here and there in the awful jumble of shattered rock were wedged the crushed and mangled forms of men, women and children.

Tears coursed down Nadara's cheeks. Sobs wracked her slender figure. And Thandar! Where was he?

With utmost difficulty the girl picked her way aloft over the tumbled debris. She could only guess at the former location of Thandar's cave, but now no sigh of cave remained — only the same blank waste of silent stone.

Frantically she tugged and tore at massive heaps of sharp edged rock. Her fingers were cut and bruised and bleeding. She called aloud the name of her man, but there was no response.

It was late in the afternoon before, weak and exhausted, she gave up her futile search. That night she slept in a crevice between two broken boulders, and the next morning she set out in search of a cave where she might live out the remainder of her lonely life in what safety and meager comfort a lone girl could wring from this savage world.

For a week she wandered hither and thither only to find most of the caves she had known in the past demolished as had been those of her people.

At last she stumbled upon the very cliff which Thandar had chosen as the permanent home of his people. Here the wrath of the earthquake seemed to have been less severe, and Nadara found, high in the cliff's face, a safe and comfortable cavern.

The last span to it required the use of a slender sapling, which she could draw up after her, effectually barring the approach of Nagoola and his people. To further protect herself against the chance of wandering men the girl carried a quantity of small bits of rock to the ledge beside the entrance to her cave.

Fruit and nuts and vegetables she took there too, and a great gourd of water from the spring below. As she completed her last trip, and sat resting upon the ledge, her eyes wandering over the landscape and out across the distant ocean, she thought she saw something move in the shadow of the trees across the open plain beneath her.

Could it have been a man? Nadara drew her sapling ladder to the ledge beside her.

*T*hurg, fleeing from the wrath of The Great Nagoola, had come at daybreak to the spot where his people had been camped, but there he found no sign of them, only the ragged edges of a great fissure, half-closed, that might have swallowed his entire tribe as he had seen the fissures in the forest swallow many, many trees at a single bite.

For some time he sought for signs of his tribesmen, but without success. Then, his fear of the earthquake allayed, he started back into the forest to find the girl. For days he sought her. He came to the ruins of the cliff that had housed her people, and there he discovered signs that the girl had been there since the demolition of the cliff.

He saw the print of her dainty foot in the soft earth at the base of the rocks — he saw how she had searched the debris for Thandar — he saw her bed of grasses in the crevice between two boulders, and then, after diligent search, he found her spoor leading away to the east.

For many days he followed her until, at last, close by the sea, he came to a level plain at the edge of a forest. Across the narrow plain rose lofty hills — and what was that clambering aloft toward the dark mouth of a cave?

Could it be the woman? Thurg's eyes narrowed as he peered intently toward the cliff. Yes, it was a woman — it was *the* woman — it was she he sought, and, she was alone.

With a whoop of exultation Thurg broke from the forest into the plain, running swiftly toward the cliff where Nadara crouched beside her little pile of jagged missiles, prepared to once more battle with this hideous monster for more than life.

VI

THE SEARCH

A year had elapsed since Waldo Emerson Smith-Jones had departed from the Back Bay home of his aristocratic parents to seek in a long sea voyage a cure for the hacking cough and hectic cheeks which had in themselves proclaimed the almost incurable.

Two months later had come the first meager press notices of the narrow escape of the steamer, upon which Waldo Emerson had been touring the south seas, from utter destruction by a huge tidal wave. The dispatch read:

> The captain reports that the great wave swept entirely over the steamer, momentarily submerging her. Two members of the crew, the officer upon the bridge, and one passenger were washed away.
>
> The latter was an American traveling for his health, Waldo E. Smith-Jones, son of John Alden Smith-Jones of Boston.
>
> The steamer came about, cruising back and forth for some time, but as the wave had washed her perilously close to a dangerous shore, it seemed unsafe to remain longer in the vicinity, for fear of a recurrence of the tidal

wave which would have meant the utter annihilation of the vessel upon the nearby beach.

No sign of any of the poor unfortunates was seen.

Mrs. Smith-Jones is prostrated.

Immediately John Alden Smith-Jones had fitted out his yacht, *Priscilla,* dispatching her under Captain Burlinghame, a retired naval officer, and an old friend of Mr. Smith-Jones, to the far distant coast in search of the body of his son, which the captain of the steamer was of the opinion might very possibly have been washed upon the beach.

And now Burlinghame was back to report the failure of his mission. The two men were sitting in the John Alden Smith-Jones library. Mrs. Smith-Jones was with them.

"We searched the beach diligently at the point opposite which the tidal wave struck the steamer," Captain Burlinghame was saying. "For miles up and down the coast we patrolled very inch of the sand."

"We found, at one spot upon the edge of the jungle and above the beach, the body of one of the sailors. It was not and could not have been Waldo's. The clothing was that of a seaman, the frame was much shorter and stockier than your son's. There was no sign of any other body along that entire coast.

"Thinking it possible one of the men might have been washed ashore alive we sent parties into the interior. Here we found a wild and savage country, and on two occasions met with fierce, white savages, who hurled rocks at us and fled at the first report of our firearms.

"We continued our search all around the island, which is of considerable extent. Upon the east coast I found this," and here the captain handed Mr. Smith-Jones the bag of jewels which Nadara had forgotten as she fled from Thandar.

Briefly he narrated what he knew of the history of the poor woman to whom it had belonged.

"I recall the incident quite well," said Mrs. Smith-Jones, "I had the pleasure of entertaining the count and countess when they stopped here upon their honeymoon. They were lovely people, and to think that they met so tragic an end!"

The three lapsed into silence. Burlinghame did not know whether he was glad or sorry that he had not found the bones of Waldo Emerson — that would have meant the end of hope for his parents. Perhaps much the same thoughts were running through the minds of the others.

Somewhere in the nether regions of the great house an electric bell sounded. Still the three sat on in silence. They heard the houseman open the front door. They heard low voices, and presently there came a deferential tap upon the door of the library.

Mr. Smith-Jones looked up and nodded. It was the houseman. He held a letter in his hand.

"What is it, Krutz?" asked the master in a tired voice. It seemed that nothing ever again would interest him.

"A special delivery letter, sir," replied the servant. "The boy says you must sign for it yourself, sir."

"Ah, yes," replied Mr. Smith-Jones as he reached for the letter and the receipt blank.

He glanced at the post mark — San Francisco.

Idly he cut the envelope.

"Pardon me?" He glanced at first his wife and then at Captain Burlinghame.

The two nodded.

Mr. John Alden Smith-Jones opened the letter. There was a single written sheet and an enclosure in another envelope. He had read but a couple of lines when he came suddenly upright in his chair.

Captain Burlinghame and Mrs. Smith-Jones looked at him in polite and surprised questioning.

"My God!" exclaimed Mr. Smith-Jones. "He is alive — Waldo is alive!"

Mrs. Smith-Jones and Captain Burlinghame sprang from their chairs and ran toward the speaker.

With trembling hands that made it difficult to read the words that his trembling voice could scarce utter John Alden Smith-Jones read aloud:

On board the Sally Corwith,
San Francisco, California.

Mr. John Alden Smith-Jones,

Boston, Mass.

Dear Sir:

Just reached port and hasten to forward letter you son gave me for his mother. He wouldn't come with us. We found him on —— Island, Lat 10° South, Long. 150° West. He seemed in good health and able to look out for himself. Didn't want anything, he said, except a razor, so we gave him that and one of the men gave him a plug of chewing tobacco. Urged him to come, but he wouldn't. The enclosed letter will doubtless tell you all about him.

Yours truly,
Henry Dobbs, Master

"Ten south, a hundred and fifty west," mused Captain Burlinghame. "That's the same island we searched. Where could he have been!"

Mrs. Smith-Jones had opened the letter addressed to her, and was reading it breathlessly.

My dear Mother:

I feel rather selfish in remaining and possibly causing you further anxiety, but I have certain duties to perform to several of the inhabitants which I feel obligated to fulfill before I depart.

My treatment here has been all that anyone might desire — even more, I might say.

The climate is delightful. My cough has left me, and I am entirely a well man — more robust than I ever recall having been in the past.

At present I am sojourning in the mountains, having but run down to the seashore today, where, happily, I chanced to find the Sally Corwith in the harbor, and am taking advantage of Captain Dobb's kindness to forward this letter to you.

Do not worry, dearest mother; my obligations will soon be fulfilled and then I shall hasten to take the first steamer for Boston.

I have met a number of interesting people here — the most interesting people I have ever met. They quite overwhelm one with their attentions.

And now, as Captain Dobbs is anxious to be away, I will
close, with every assurance of my deepest love for you and father.
Ever affectionately your son,
Waldo

Mrs. Smith-Jones' eyes were dim with tears — tears of thanksgiving and happiness.

"And to think," she exclaimed, "that after all he is alive and well — quite well. His cough has left him — that is the best part of it, and he is surrounded by interesting people — just what Waldo needed. For some time I feared, before he sailed, that he was devoting himself too closely to his studies and to the little côterie of our own set which surrounded him. This experience will be broadening. Of course these people may be slightly provincial, but it is evident that they posses a certain culture and refinement — otherwise my Waldo would never have described them as 'interesting.' The coarse, illiterate, or vulgar could never prove 'interesting' to a Smith-Jones."

Captain Cecil Burlinghame nodded politely — he was thinking of the naked, hairy man-brutes he had seen within the interior of the island.

"It is evident, Burlinghame," said Mr. Smith-Jones, "that you overlooked a portion of the island. It would seem, from Waldo's letter, there must be a colony of civilized men and women upon it. Of course it is possible that it may be further inland than you penetrated."

Burlinghame shook his head.

"I am puzzled," he said. "We circled the entire coast, yet nowhere did we see any evidence of a man-improved harbor, such as one might have reason to expect were there really a colony of advanced humans in the interior. There would have been at least a shack near the beach in one of the several natural harbors which indent the coast line was there even an occasional steamer touching for purposes of commerce with the colonists.

"No, my friends," he continued, "as much as I should like to believe it my judgment will not permit me to place any such translation upon Waldo's letter.

"That he is safe and happy seems evident, and that is enough for us to know. Now it should be a simple matter for us to find him — if it is still your desire to send for him."

"He may already have left for Boston," said Mrs. Smith-Jones; "his letter was written several months ago."

Again Burlinghame shook his head.

"Do not back on that, my dear madam," he said kindly. "It may be fifty years before another vessel touches that forgotten shore — unless it be one which your yourselves send."

John Alden Smith-Jones sprang to his feet, and commenced pacing up and down the library.

"How soon can the *Priscilla* be put in shape to make the return voyage to the island?" he asked.

"It *can* be done in a week, if necessary," replied Burlinghame.

"And you will accompany her, in command?"

"Gladly."

"Good!" exclaimed Mr. Smith-Jones. "And now, my friend, let us lose no time in starting our preparations. I intend accompanying you."

"And I shall go too," said Mrs. Smith-Jones.

The two men looked at her in surprise.

"But my dear!" cried her husband, "there is no telling what hardships and dangers we may encounter — you could never stand such a trip."

"I am going," said Mrs. Smith-Jones, firmly. "I know my Waldo. I know his refined and sensitive nature. I know that I am fully capable of enduring whatever he may have endured. He tells me that he is among interesting people. Evidently there is nothing to fear, then, from the inhabitants of the island, and furthermore I wish personally to meet the people he has been living with. I have always been careful to surround Waldo with only the nicest people, and if any vulgarizing influences have been brought to bear upon him since he has been beyond my mature guidance I wish to know it, that I may determine how to combat their results."

That was the end of it. If Mrs. Smith-Jones knew her son, Mr. Smith-Jones certainly knew his wife.

A week later the *Priscilla* sailed from Boston harbor on her long journey around the Horn to the south seas.

Most of the old crew had been retained. The first and second officers were new men. The former, William Stark, had come to the Burlinghame well recommended. From the first he seemed an intelligent and experienced officer. That he was inclined to taciturnity but enhanced his value in the eyes of Burlinghame. Stark was including to be something of a martinet, so that the crew soon took to hating him cordially, but as his display of this unpleasant trait was confined wholly to trivial acts the men contended themselves with grumbling among themselves, which is the prerogative and pleasure of every good sailorman. Their loyalty to the splendid Burlinghame, however, was not to be shaken by even a dozen Starks.

The monotonous and uneventful journey to the vicinity of ten south and a hundred and fifty west was finally terminated. At last land showed on the starboard bow. Excitement reigned supreme throughout the trim, white *Priscilla*. Mrs. Smith-Jones peered anxiously and almost constantly through her binoculars, momentarily expecting to see the well-known thin and emaciated figure of her Waldo Emerson standing upon the beach awaiting them.

For two weeks they sailed along the coast, stopping here and there for a day while parties tramped inland in search of signs of civilized habitation. They lay two days in the harbor where the *Sally Corwith* had lain. There they pressed farther inland than at any other point, but all without avail. It was Burlinghame's plan to first make a cursory survey of the entire coast, with only short incursions toward the center of the island. Should this fail to discover the missing Waldo the part was then to go over the ground once more, remaining weeks or months as might be required to thoroughly explore every foot of the island.

It was during the pursuit of the initial portion of the program that they dropped anchor in the self-same harbor upon whose waters Waldo Emerson and Nadara had seen the *Priscilla* lying, only to fly from her.

Burlinghame recalled it as the spot at which the bag of jewels had been picked up. Next to the *Sally Corwith* harbor, has they had come to call the other anchorage, this seemed most fraught with possibilities of success. They christened it Eugénie Bay, after that poor, unfortunate lady, Eugénie Marie Céleste de la Valois, Countess of Crecy, whose jewels had been recovered upon its shore.

Burlinghame and Waldo's father with half a dozen officers and men of the *Priscilla* had spent the day searching the woods, the plain and the hills for some slight sign of human habitation. Shortly after noon First Officer Stark stumbled upon the whitened skeleton of a man. In answer to his shouts the other members of the party hastened to his side. They found the grim thing lying in a little barren spot among the tall grasses. About it the liquids of decomposition had killed vegetation leaving the thing all alone in all its grisly repulsiveness as though shocked, nature had withdrawn in terror.

Star stood pointing toward it without a word as the others came up. Burlinghame was the firs tot reach Stark's side. He bent low over the bones examining the skull carefully. John Alden Smith-Jones came panting up. Instantly he saw what Burlinghame was examining he turned deathly white. Burlinghame looked up at him.

"It's not," he said. "Look at that skull — either a gorilla or some very low type of man."

Mr. Smith-Jones breathed a sigh of relief.

"What an awful creature it must have been," he said, when he had fully taken in the immense breadth of the squat skeleton. "It cannot be that Waldo has survived in a wilderness people by such creatures as this. Imagine him confronted by such a beast. Timid by nature and never robust he would have perished of fright at the very sight of this thing charging down upon him."

Captain Cecil Burlinghame acquiesced with a nod. He knew Waldo Emerson well and so he could not even imagine a meeting between the frail and cowardly youth and such a beast as this bleaching frame must once have supported. And at their feet the bones of Flatfoot lay mute witness to the impossible.

Presently a shout from one of the sailors attracted their attention toward the far side of the valley. The man was gesticulating violently toward the lofty cliffs which rose sheer from the rank jungle grasses. All eyes turned in the direction indicated by the excited sailor. At first they saw nothing, but presently a figure came in sight upon a little elevation. It was the figure of a human being, and even at the distance they were from it all were assured that it was the figure of a female. She was running toward the cliffs with the speed of a deer. And now, behind her, came another figure. thickset and squat was the thing that pursued the woman. It might have been the reanimated skeleton they had just discovered.

Would the creature catch her before she reached the cliff? Would she find sanctuary even there? Already Burlinghame and Stark had started toward the cliff on a run. John Alden Smith-Jones followed more slowly. The men raced after their officers.

The girl had reached the rocks and was scampering up their precipitous face like a squirrel. Close behind her came the man. They saw the girl reach a ledge just below the mouth of a cave in which she evidently expected to find safety. They saw her clambering up the rickety sapling that answered for a ladder. They breathed sighs of relief, for it seemed that she was now quite safe — the man was still one ledge below her.

But in another moment the watchers were filled with horror. The brute pursuing her had reached forth a giant hand and seized the base of the sapling. He was dragging it over the edge of the cliff. In another moment the girl would be precipitated either into his arms or to a horrible death upon the jagged rocks beneath her.

Burlinghame and Stark halted simultaneously. At once two rifles leaped to their shoulders. There were two reports, so close together they seemed as one.

VII

FIRST MATE STARK

*U*pon the day that Thurg discovered Nadara he had come racing to the foot of the cliff, roaring and bellowing like a mad bull. Upward he clambered half the distance to the girl's lofty perch. Then a bit of jagged rock, well aimed, had brought him to a sudden halt, spitting blood and teeth from his injured mouth. He looked up at Nadara and shrieked out his rage and his threats of vengeance. Nadara launched another missile at him that caught him full upon one eye, dropping him like a stone to the narrow ledge upon which he had been standing. Quickly the girl started to descend to this side to finish the work she had commenced, for she knew that there could be no peace or safety for her, now that Thurg had discovered her hiding place, while the monster lived.

But she had scare more than lowered her sapling to the ledge beneath her when the giant form of the man moved and Thurg sat up. Quickly Nadara clambered back to her ledge, again drawing her sapling after her. She was about to hurl another missile at the man when he spoke to her.

"We are all alone in the world," he said. "All your people and all my people have been slain by the Great Nagoola. Come down. Let us live together in peace. There is no other left in all the world."

Nadara laughed at him.

"Come down to you!" she cried, mockingly. "Live with you! I would rather live with the pigs that root in the forest. Go away, or I will finish what I have commenced, and kill you. I would not live with you though I knew that you were the last human being on earth."

Thurg pleaded and threatened, but all to no avail. Again he tried to clamber to her side, but again he was repulsed with well-aimed missiles. At last he withdrew, growling and threatening.

For weeks he haunted the vicinity of the cliff. Nadara's meager food supply was soon exhausted. She was forced to descend to replenish her larder and fill her gourd, or die of starvation and thirst. She made her trips to the forest at night, though black Nagoola prowled and the menace of Thurg looked through the darkness. At last the man discovered her in one of these nocturnal expeditions and almost caught her before she reached her ledge of safety.

For three days he kept her a close prisoner. Again her stock of provisions were exhausted. She was desperate. Twice had Nagoola nearly trapped her in the forest. She dared not again tempt fate in the gloomy wood by night. There was nothing left but to risk all in one last effort to elude Thurg by day and find another asylum in some far distant corner of the island.

Carefully she watched her opportunity, and while the beast-man was temporarily absent seeking food for himself the girl slid swiftly to the base of the cliff and started through the tall grasses for the opposite side of the valley.

Upon this day Thurg had fallen upon the spoor of deer as he had searched the forest for certain berries that were in season and which he particularly enjoyed. The trail led along the edge of the wood to the opposite side of the valley, and over the hills into the region beyond. All day Thurg followed the fleet animals, until at last not having come up with them he was forced to give up the pursuit and return to the cliffs, lest his more valuable quarry should escape.

Halfway between the hills and the cliff he came suddenly face to face with Nadara. Not twenty paces separated them. With a howl of satisfaction Thurg leaped to seize her, but she turned and fled before he could lay his hand upon her. If Thurg had found his other quarry of that day swift, so, too, he now found Nadara, for terror gave wings to her flying feet. Lumbering after her came Thurg, and had the distance been less he would have been left far behind, but it was a long distance from the spot, where they had met, to Nadara's cliffs. The girl could out-run the man for a short distance, but when victory depended upon endurance the advantage was all on the side of the brute.

As they neared the goal Nadara realized that the lead she had gained at first was rapidly being overcome by the horrid creatures panting so close behind her. She strained every nerve and muscle in a last mad effort to distance the fate that was closing upon her. She reached the cliff. Thurg was just behind her. Half spent, she stumbled upward in, what seemed to her, pitiful slowness. At last her hand grasped the sapling that led to the mouth of her cave — in another instant she would be safe. But her newborn hope went out as she felt the sapling slipping and glanced downward to see Thurg dragging it from its position.

She shut her eyes that she might not see the depths below into which she was about to be hurled, and then there smote upon her ears the most terrific burst of sound that had ever assailed them, other than the thunders that rolled down out of the heavens when the rains came. But this sound did not come from above — it came from the valley beneath.

The ladder ceased to slip. She opened her eyes and glanced downward. Far below her lay the body of Thurg. She could see that he was quite dead. He lay upon his face and from his back trickled two tiny streams of blood from little holes.

Nadara clambered upward to her ledge, drawing her sapling after her, and then she looked about for an explanation of the strange noise and the sudden death of Thurg, for she could not but connect the one with the other. Below, in the valley, she saw a number of men strangely garbed. They were coming toward her cliff. She gathered her missiles closely about her, ready to her hand. Now they were below and calling up to her. Her eyes dilated in wonder — they spoke the strange tongue that Thandar had tried to teach her. She called down to them in her own tongue, but they shook their heads, motioning her to descend. She was afraid. All her life she had been afraid of men, and with reason — of all except her old foster father and Thandar. These, evidently, were men. She could only expect from them the same treatment that Thurg would have accorded her.

One of them had started up the face of the cliff. It was Stark. Nadara seized a bit of rock and hurled it down upon him. He barely dodged the missile, but he desisted in his attempt to ascend to her. Now Burlinghame advanced, raising his hand, palm toward her in sign that she should not assault him. She recalled some of the language that Thandar had taught her — maybe they would understand it.

"Go-away!" she cried. "Go-away! Nadara kill bad-men."

A look of pleasure overspread Burlinghame's face — the girl spoke English.

"We are not bad men," he called up to her. "We will not harm you."

"What do you want?" Asked Nadara, still unconvinced by mere words.

"We want to talk with you," replied Burlinghame. "We are looking for a friend who was ship-wrecked upon this island. Come down. We will not harm you. Have we not already proved our friendship by killing this fellow who pursued you?"

This man spoke precisely the tongue of Thandar. Nadara could understand every word, for Thandar had talked to her much in English. She could understand it better than she could speak it. If they talked the same tongue as Thandar they must be from the same country. Maybe they were Thandar's friends. Anyway, they were like him, and Thandar had never harmed women. She could trust them. Slowly she lowered her sapling and began the descent. Several times she hesitated as though minded to return to her ledge, but Burlinghame's kindly voice and encouragement at last prevailed, and presently Nadara stood before them.

The officers and men of the *Priscilla* crowded around the girl. They were struck by her beauty, and the simple dignity of her manner and her carriage. The great black panther skin that fell from her left shoulder she wore with the majesty of a queen and with a naturalness that cast no reflection upon her modesty, though it revealed quite as much of her figure as it hid. William Stark, first officer of the *Priscilla*, caught his breath — never, he was positive, had God made a more lovely creature.

From the top of the cliff a shaggy man peered down upon the strange scene. He blinked his little eyes, scratched his matted head, and once he picked up a large stone that lay near him; but he did not hurl it upon those below, for he had heard the loud report of the rifles, seen the smoke belch from the muzzles, and witnessed the sudden and miraculous collapse of Thurg.

Burlinghame was speaking to Nadara.

"Who are you?" he asked the girl.

"Nadara," replied the girl.

"Where do you live?"

Nadara jerked her thumb over her shoulder toward the cliff at her back. Burlinghame searched the rocky escarpment with his eyes, but saw no sign of another living being there.

"Where are your people?"

"Dead."

"All of them?"

Nadara nodded affirmatively.

"How long have they been dead and what killed them?" continued Burlinghame.

"Almost a moon. The Great Nagoola killed them."

In answer to other questions Nadara related all that had transpired since the night of the earthquake. Her description of the catastrophe convinced the Americans that a violent quake had recently occurred to shake the island to its foundations.

"Ask her about Waldo," whispered Mr. Smith-Jones, himself dreading the question.

"We are looking for a young man," said Burlinghame, "who was lost overboard from a steamer on the west coast of this island. We know that he reached the shore alive, for we have heard from him. Have you ever seen or heard of this stranger? His name is Waldo Emerson Smith-Jones — this gentleman is his father," indicated Mr. Smith-Jones.

Nadara looked with wide eyes at John Alden Smith-Jones. So this man was Thandar's father. She felt very sorry for him, for she knew that he loved Thandar — Thandar had often told her so. She did not know how to tell him — she shrank from causing another the anguish and misery that she had endured.

"Did you know of him?" asked Burlinghame.

Nadara nodded her head.

"Where is he?" cried Waldo's father. "Where are the people with whom he lived here?"

Nadara came close to John Alden Smith-Jones. There was no fear in her innocent young heart for this man who was Thandar's father — who loved Thandar — only a great compassion for him in the sorrow that she was about to inflict. Gently she took his hand in hers, raising her sad eyes to his.

"Where is he? Where is my boy?" whispered Mr. Smith-Jones.

"He is with his people, who were my people — the people of whom I have just told you," replied Nadara softly — "He is dead." And then she dropped her face upon the man's hand and wept.

The shock staggered John Alden Smith-Jones. It seemed incredible — impossible — that Waldo could have lived through all that he must have lived through to perish at last but a few short weeks before succor reached him. For a moment he forgot the girl. It was her hot tears upon his hand that aroused him to a consciousness of the present.

"Why do you weep?" he cried almost roughly.

"For you," she replied, "who loved him, too."

"You loved Waldo?" asked the boy's father.

Nadara nodded her tumbled mass of raven hair. John Alden Smith-Jones looked down upon the bent head of the sobbing girl in silence for several minutes. Many things were racing through his patrician brain. He was by training, environment and heredity narrow and Puritanical. He saw the meager apparel of the girl — he saw her nut brown skin; but he did not see her nakedness, for something in his heart told him that sweet virtue clothed her more effectively and could silks and satins without virtue. Gently he placed an arm about her, drawing her to him.

"My daughter," he said, and pressed his lips to her forehead.

It was a solemn and sorrow-ridden party that boarded the *Priscilla* an hour later. Mrs. Smith-Jones had seen them coming. Some intuitive sense may have warned her of the sorrow that lay in store for her upon their return. At any rate, she did not meet them at the rail as in the past, instead she returned to her cabin to await her husband there. When he joined her he brought with him a half-naked young woman. Mrs. Smith-Jones looked upon the girl with ill concealed horror.

Waldo's mother met the shock of her husband's news with much greater fortitude than he had expected. As a matter of fact she had been prepared for this from the first. She had never really believed that Waldo could survive for any considerable time far from the comforts and luxuries of his Boston home and the watchful care of herself.

"And who is this — ah — person?" she asked coldly at last, holding her *pince-nez* before her eyes as with elevated brows she cast a look of disapproval upon Nadara.

The girl, reading more in the older woman's manner than her words, drew herself up proudly. Mr. Smith-Jones coughed and colored. He stepped to Nadara's side, placing her arm about her shoulders.

"She loved Waldo," he said simply.

"The brazen hussy!" exclaimed Mrs. Smith-Jones. "To dare love a Smith-Jones!"

"Come, come, Louisa!" ejaculated her husband. "Remember that she too is suffering — do not add to her sorrow. She loved our boy, and he returned her love."

"How do you know that?"

"She has told me," replied the man.

"It is not true," cried Mrs. Smith-Jones. "It is not true! Waldo Emerson would never stoop to love one out of his own high class. Who is she, and what proof have you that Waldo loved her?"

"I am Nadara," said the girl proudly, answering for herself. "And this is the proof that he loved me. He told me that this was the pledge token between us until we could come to his land and be mated according to the customs there." She held out her left hand, upon the third finger of which sparkled a great solitaire — a solitaire which Mrs. John Alden Smith-Jones recognized instantly.

"He gave you that?" she asked.

Then she turned toward her husband.

"What do you intend doing with this girl?" she asked.

"I shall take her back home," replied he. "She should be as a daughter to us, for Waldo would have made her such had he lived. She cannot remain upon the island. All her people were killed by the earthquake that destroyed Waldo. She is in constant danger of attack by the wild beasts and wilder men. We cannot leave her here, and even if we could I should not do so, for we owe a duty to our dead boy to care for her as he would have cared for her — and we owe a greater duty to her."

"I must be alone," was all that Mrs. Smith-Jones replied. "Please take her away, John. Give her the cabin next to this, and have Marie clothe her properly — Marie's clothes should about fit her." There was more of tired anguish in her voice now than of anger.

Mr. Smith-Jones led Nadara out and summoned Marie, but Nadara upset his plans by announcing that she wished to return to the shore.

"She does not like me," she said, nodding toward Mrs. Smith-Jones's cabin, "and I will not stay."

It took John Alden Smith-Jones a long time to persuade the girl to change her mind. He pointed out that his wife was greatly overwrought by the shock of the news of Waldo's death. He assured Nadara that at heart she was a kindly woman, and that eventually she would regret her attitude toward the girl. And at last Nadara consented to remain aboard the *Priscilla*. But when Marie would have clothed her in the garments of civilization she absolutely refused — scorning the hideous and uncomfortable clothing.

It was two days before Mrs. Smith-Jones sent for her. When she entered that lady's cabin the latter exclaimed at once against her barbarous attire.

"I gave instructions that Marie should dress you properly," she said. "You are not decently clothed — that bear skin is shocking."

Nadara tossed her head, and her eyes flashed fire.

"I shall never wear your silly clothes," she cried. "This Thandar gave me — he slew Nagoola, the black panther, with his own hands, and gave the skin to me who was to be his mate — do you think I would exchange it for such foolish garments as these?" she waved a contemptuous gesture toward Mrs. Smith-Jones expensive morning gown.

The elder woman forgot her outraged dignity in the suggestion the girl had given her for an excuse to be rid of her at the first opportunity. She had mentioned a party named Thandar. She had brazenly boasted that this Thandar had killed the beast whose pelt she wore and had given her the thing for a garment. She had admitted that she was to become this person's "mate." Mrs. Smith-Jones shuddered at the primitive word. At this moment Mr. Smith-Jones entered the cabin. He smiled pleasantly at Nadara, and then, seeing in the attitudes of the two women that he had stepped within a theater of war, he looked questioningly at his wife.

"Now what, Louisa?" he asked, somewhat sharply.

"Sufficient, John," exclaimed that lady, "to bear out my original contention that it was a very unwise move to bring this woman with us — she has just admitted that she was the promised 'mate' of a person she calls Thandar. She is brazen — I refuse to permit her to enter my home; nor shall she remain upon the *Priscilla* longer than is necessary to land her at the first civilized port."

Mr. Smith-Jones looked questioningly at Nadara. The girl had guessed the erroneous reasoning that had caused Mrs. Smith-Jones's excitement. She had forgotten that they did not know that Waldo and Thandar were one. Now she could scarce repress a smile of amusement nor resist the temptation to take advantage of Mrs. Smith-Jones's ignorance to bait her further.

"You had another lover beside Waldo?" asked Mr. Smith-Jones.

"I loved Thandar," she replied. "Thandar was king of my people. He loved me. He slew Nagoola for me and gave me his skin. He slew Korth and Flatfoot, also. They wanted me, but Thandar slew them. And Big Fist he slew, and Sag the Killer — oh, Thandar was a mighty fighter. Can you wonder that I loved him?"

"He was a hideous murderer!" cried Mrs. Smith-Jones, "and to think that my poor Waldo; poor, timid, gentle Waldo, was condemned to live among such savage brutes. Oh, it is too terrible!"

Nadara's eyes went wide. It was her turn to suffer a shock. "Poor, timid, gentle Waldo!" Had she heard aright? Could it be that they were describing the same man? There must be some mistake.

"Did Waldo know that you loved Thandar?" asked Mr. Smith-Jones.

"Thandar was Waldo," she replied. "Thandar is the name I gave him — it means the Brave One. He was very brave," she cried. "He was not 'timid,' and he was only 'gentle' with women and children."

Mrs. Smith-Jones had never been so shocked in all her life. She sprang to her feet.

"Leave my cabin!" she cried. "I see through your shallow deception. You thoughtlessly betrayed yourself and your vulgar immoralities, and now you try to hide behind a base calumny that pictures my dear, dead boy as one with your hideous, brutal chief. You shall not deceive me longer. Leave my cabin, please!"

Mr. Smith-Jones stood as one paralyzed. He could not believe in the perfidy of the girl — it seemed impossible that she could have so deceived him — nor yet could he question the integrity of his own ears. It was, of course, too far beyond the pale of reason to attempt to believe that Waldo Emerson and the terrible Thandar were one and the same. The girl had gone too far, and yet he could not believe that she was bad. There must be some explanation.

In the meantime Nadara had left the room, her little chin high in the air. Never again, she determined, would she subject herself to the insults of Thandar's mother. She went on deck. She craved the fresh air, and the excitement to be found above. The officers had been very nice to her. Stark was much with her. The man had fallen desperately in love with the half-savage girl. As she reached the deck after leaving Mrs. Smith-Jones's cabin Stark was the first she chanced to meet. She would have preferred being alone with her sorrow and her anger, but the man joined her. Together they stood by the rail watching the approach of heavy clouds. A storm was about to break over them that had been brewing for several days.

Stark knew nothing of what had taken place below, but he saw that the girl was unhappy. He attempted to cheer her. At last he took her hand and stoked it caressingly as he talked with her. Before she could guess his intention he was pouring words of love and passion into her ears. Nadara drew away. A puzzled expression contracted her brows.

"Do not talk so to Nadara," she said. "She does not love you." And then she moved away and went to her cabin.

Stark looked after her as she departed. He was thoroughly aroused. Who was this savage girl, to repulse him? What would have been her fate for his well-directed shot? Was not the man who had been pursuing her but acting after the customs of her wild people? He would have taken her by force. That was the only way she would have been taken had she been left upon her own island. That was the only kind of betrothal she knew. It was what she expected. He had been a fool to approach her with the soft words of civilization. They had made her despise him. She should have understood force and loved him for it. Well, he would show her that he could be as primitive as any of her savage lovers.

*T*he storm broke. The wind became a hurricane. The *Priscilla* was forced to turn and flee before the anger of the elements, so that she retraced her course of the past two days and then was blown to the north.

Stark saw nothing of Nadara during this period. At the end of thirty-six hours the wind had died and the sea was settling to its normal quiet. It was the first evening after the storm. The deck of the *Priscilla* was almost deserted. The yacht was moving slowly along not far off the shore of one of the many islands that dot that part of the south seas.

Nadara came on deck for a walk before retiring. Stark and two other sailors were on watch. At sight of the girl the first officer approached her. He spoke pleasantly as though nothing had occurred to mar their friendly relations. He talked of the storm and pointed out the black outlines of the nearby shore, and as he talked he led her toward the stern, out of sight of the sailors forward.

Suddenly he turned upon her and grasped her into his arms. With brutal force he crushed her to him, covering her face with kisses. She fought to free herself, but Stark was a strong man. Slowly he forced her to the deck. She beat him in the face and upon the breast, and at last, in the extreme of desperation, she screamed for help. Instantly he struck her a heavy blow upon the jaw. The slender form of the girl relaxed upon the deck in unconsciousness.

Now Stark came to a sudden realization of the gravity of the thing he had done. He knew that when Nadara regained consciousness his perfidy would come to the attention of Captain Burlinghame, and he feared the quiet, ex-naval officer more than he did the devil. He looked over the rail. It would be an easy thing to dispose of the girl. He had only to drop her unconscious body into the still waters below. He raised her in his arms and bore her to the rail. The moon shone down upon her face. He looked out over the water and saw the shore so close at hand.

There would be a thorough investigation and the sailors, who had no love for him, as he well knew, would lose no time in reporting that he had been the last to be seen with the girl. Evidently he was in for it, one way or the other.

Again he looked down into Nadara's face. She was very beautiful. He wanted her badly. Slowly his glance wandered to the calm waters of the ocean and on to the quiet shore line. Then back to the girl. For a moment he stood irresolute. Then he stepped to the side of the cabin where hung a life preserver to which was attached a long line.

He put the life preserver about Nadara. Then he lowered her into the ocean. The moment he felt her weight transferred from the lowering rope to the life preserver he vaulted over the yacht's rail into the dark waters beneath her stern.

VIII

THE WILD MEN

Nadara did not regain consciousness until Stark had reached shore and was dragging her out upon the beach above the surf. For several minutes after she had opened her eyes she had difficulty in recalling the events that had immediately preceded Stark's attack upon her. She felt the life belt still about her, and as Stark stopped above her to remove it she knew that it was he though she could not distinguish his features.

What had happened? Slowly a realization of the man's bold act forced itself upon her — he had leaped overboard from the *Priscilla* and swam ashore with her rather than face the consequences of his brutal conduct toward her.

To the girl reared within the protective influences of civilization Nadara's position would have seemed hopeless; but Nadara knew naught of other protection than that afforded by her own quick wits and the agility of her swift young muscles. To her it would have seemed infinitely more appalling to have been confined within the narrow limits of the yacht with this man, for there all was strange and new. She still had half feared and mistrusted all aboard the *Priscilla* except Thandar's father and Captain Burlinghame; but would they have protected her from Stark? She did not know. Among her own people only a father, brother, or mate protected a woman from one who sought her against her will, and of these she had not upon the little vessel.

But now it was different. Intuitively she knew that upon a savage shore, however strange and unfamiliar it might be, she would have every advantage over the first office of the *Priscilla*. His life had been spent close to the haunts of civilization; he knew nothing of the woodcraft that was second nature to her; he might perish in a land of plenty through ignorance of where to search for food, and of what was edible and what was not. This much her early experience with Waldo Emerson had taught her. When their paths first had crossed Waldo had been as ignorant as a newborn babe in the craft of life primeval — Nadara had had to teach him everything.

Behind them Nadara heard the gentle sloughing of trees — the myriad noises of the teeming jungle night — and she smiled. It was inky black about them. Stark had removed the life belt and placed it beneath the girl's head. He thought her still unconscious — perhaps dead. Now he was wringing the water from his clothes; his back toward her.

Nadara rose to her feet — noiseless as Nagoola. Like a shadow she melted into the blackness of the jungle that fringed the shore. Careful and alert, she picked her way within the tangled mass for a few yards. At the bole of a large tree she halted, listening. Then she made a low, weird sound with her lips, listening again for a moment after. This she repeated thrice, and then, seemingly satisfied that no danger lurked above, she swung herself into the low-hanging branches, quickly ascending until she found a comfortable seat where she might rest in ease.

Down upon the beach Stark, having wrung the surplus water from his garments, turned to examine and revive the girl, if she still lived. Even in the darkness her form had been plainly visible against the yellow sand, but now she was not there. Stark was dumfounded. His eyes leaped quickly from one point to another, yet nowhere could they discover the girl. There was the beach, the sea and the jungle. Which had she chose for her flight? It did not take Stark long to guess, and immediately he turned his steps toward the shapeless, gloomy mass that marked the forest's edge.

As he approached he went more slowly. The thought of entering that forbidding wood sent cold shivers creeping through him. Could a mere girl have dared its nameless horrors? She must have, and with the decision came new resolution. What a girl had dared certainly he might dare. Again he strode briskly toward the jungle.

Just at its verge he heard a low, weird sound not a dozen paces within the black, hideous tangle. It was Nadara voicing the two notes which some ancient forebearer of her tribe had discovered would wring an answering growl from Nagoola, and an uneasy hiss from that other arch enemy of man — the great, slimy serpent whose sinuous coils twined threateningly above them in the breaches of the trees. Only these Nadara feared — these and man. So, before entering a tree at night it was her custom to assure herself that neither Nagoola nor Coovra lurked in the branches of the tree she had chose for sanctuary. Stark beat a hasty retreat, nor did he again venture from the beach during the balance of the long, dismal night.

When dawn broke it found Nadara much refreshed by the sleep she had enjoyed within the comparative safety of the great tree, and Stark haggard and exhausted by a sleepless night of terror and regret. He cursed himself, the girl and his bestial passion, and then as his thoughts conjured her lovely face and perfect figure before his mind's eye, he leaped to his feet and swung briskly toward the jungle. He would find her. All that he had sacrificed should not be in vain. He would find her and keep her. Together they would make a home upon this tropical shore. He would get everything out of life that there was to get.

He had taken but a few steps before he discovered, plain in the damp sand before him, the prints of Nadara's naked feet in a well defined trail leading toward the wood. With a smile of satisfaction and victory the man followed it into the maze of vegetation, dank and gloomy even beneath the warm light of the morning sun.

By chance he stumbled directly upon Nadara. She had descended from her tree to search for water. They saw each other simultaneously. The girl turned and fled farther into the forest. Close behind her came the man. For several hundred yards the chase led through the thick jungle which terminated abruptly at the edge of a narrow, rock-covered clearing beyond which loomed sheer, precipitous cliffs, raising their lofty heads three hundred feet above the forest.

A half smile touched Stark's lips as he saw the barrier that nature had placed in the path of his quarry; but almost instantly it froze into an expression of horror as a slight noise to his right attracted his attention from the girl fleeing before him. For an instant he stood bewildered, then a quick glance toward the girl revealed her scaling the steep cliff with the agility of a monkey, and with a cry to attract her attention he leaped after her once more, but this time himself the quarry — the hunter become the hunted, for after him raced a score of painted savages, brandishing long, slim spears, or waving keen edged parangs.

Nadara had not needed Stark's warning cry to apprise her of the proximity of the wild men. She had seen them the instant that she cleared the jungle, and with the sight of them she knew that she need no longer harbor fear of the white man. In them, though, she saw a graver danger for herself, since they , doubtless, would have little difficulty in overhauling her in their own haunts, while she had not had much cause for worry as to her ability to elude the white man indefinitely.

Part way up the cliffs she paused to look back. Stark had reached the foot of the lowering escarpment a short distance ahead of his pursuers. He had chosen this route because of the ease with which the girl had clambered up the rocky barrier, but he had reckoned without taking into consideration the lifetime of practice which lay back of Nadara's agility. From earliest infancy she had lived upon the face and within the caves of steep cliffs. Her first toddling, baby footsteps had been along the edge of narrow shelving ledges.

When the man reached the cliff, however, he found confronting him an apparently unscalable wall. He cast a frightened, appealing glance at the girl far above him. Twice he essayed to scramble out of reach of the advancing savages, whose tattooed faces, pendulous slit ears, and sharp filed, blackened teeth lent to them a more horrid aspect than even that imparted by their murderous weapons or warlike whoops and actions. Each time he slipped back, clutching frantically at rocky projects and such hardy vegetation as had found foothold in the crevices of the granite. His hands were torn and bleeding, his face scratched and his clothing rent. And now the savages were upon him. They had seen that he was unarmed. No need as yet for spear or parang — they would take him alive.

And the girl. They had watched her in amazement as she clambered swiftly up the steep ascent. With all their primitive accomplishments this was beyond even them. They were a forest people and a river people. They dwelt in thatched houses raised high upon long piles. They knew little or nothing of the arts of the cliff dwellers. To them the feat of this strange, white girl was little short of miraculous.

Nadara saw them seize roughly upon the terror-stricken Stark. She saw them bind his hands behind his back, and then she saw them turn their attention once more toward herself.

Three of the warriors attempted to scale the cliff after her. Slowly they ascended. She smiled at their manifest fear and their awkwardness — she need have no fear of these, they never could reach her. She permitted them to approach within a dozen feet of her and then, loosening a bit of the crumbling granite, she hurled it full at the head of the foremost. With a yell of pain and terror he toppled backward upon those below him, the three tumbling, screaming and pawing to the rocks at the base of the cliff.

None of them was killed, through all were badly bruised, and he who had received her missile bled profusely from a wound upon his forehead. Their fellows laughed at them — it was scant comfort they received for being bested by a girl. Then they withdrew a short distance, and squatting in a circle they commenced a lengthy palaver. Their repeated gestures in her direction convinced Nadara that she was the subject of their debate.

Presently one of their number arose and approached the foot of the cliff. There he harangued the girl for several minutes. When he was done he awaited, evidently for a reply from her; but as Nadara had not been able to understand a word of the fellow's language she could but shake her head.

The spokesman returned to his fellow and once again a length council was held. During it Nadara climbed farther aloft, that she might be out of range of the slender spears. Upon a narrow ledge she halted, gathering about her such loose bits of rock as she could dislodge from the face of the cliff — she would be prepared for a sudden onslaught, nor for a moment did she doubt the outcome of the battle. She felt that but for the lack of food and water she could hold this cliff face forever against innumerable savages — could they climb no better than these.

But the wild men did not again attempt to storm her citadel. Instead they leaped suddenly from their council, and without a glance toward her disappeared in the forest, taking their prisoner with them. Out of sight of the girl, they stationed two of their number just within the screening verdure to capture the girl should she descend. The others hastened parallel with the cliff until a sudden turn inland took them to a point from which they could again emerge into the clearing out of the sight of Nadara.

Here they took immediately to a well-worn path that led back and forth upward across the face of the cliff. Stark was dragged and prodded forward with them in their ascent. Sharp spears and the points of keen parangs urged him to haste. By the time the party reached the summit the white man was bleeding from a score of superficial wounds.

Now the part turned back along the top of the bluff in the direction from which they had come.

Nadara, unable to fathom their reason for having abandoned the attempt to capture her, was, however, not lulled into any feeling of false security. She knew the cliff was the safest place for her, and yet the pangs of thirst and hunger warned her that she must soon leave it to seek sustenance. She was about to descend to the jungle below in search of food and water, when the faintest of movements of earth sweeping creepers depending from a giant buttress tree below her and just within the verge of the forest arrested her acute attention. She knew that the movement had been caused by some animal beneath the tree, and finally, as she watched intently for a moment or two, she descried an Argus pheasant with which the war caps of the savages had been adorned.

Though she knew now that she was watched, she also knew that she could reach the top of the cliff and possibly find both food and drink, if it chanced to be near, before the savages could overtake her. Then she must depend upon her wits and her speed to regain the safety of the cliff ahead of them. That they would attempt to scale the barrier at the same point at which she climbed it she doubted, for she had seen that they were comparatively unaccustomed to this sort of going, and so she guessed that if they followed her upward at all it would be by means of some beaten trail of which they had knowledge.

And so Nadara scaled the heights, passing over and around obstacles that would have blanched the cheek of the hardiest mountain climber, with the ease and speed of the chamois. At the summit she found a open, parklike forest, and into this she plunged, running forward in quest of food and drink. A few familiar fruits and nuts assuaged the keenest pangs of hunger, but nowhere could she find water or signs of water.

She had traveled for almost a mile, directly inland from the coast, when she stumbled, purely by chance, upon a little spring hidden in a leafy bower. The cool, clear water refreshed her, imparting to her new life and energy. After drinking her fill she sought some means of carrying a little supply of the priceless liquid back to her cliff side refuge, but though she searched diligently she could discover no growing thing that might be transformed into a vessel.

There as nothing for it then other than to return, without the water, trusting to her wits to find the means of eluding the savages from time to time as it became necessary for her to quench her thirst. Later, she was sure, she should discover some form of gourd, or the bladder of an animal in which she could hoard a few precious drops.

Her woodcraft, combined with her almost uncanny sense of direction, led her directly back to the spot at which she had topped he cliff. There was no sign of the savages. She breathed a sigh of relief as she stepped to the edge of the forest, and then, all about her, from behind trees and bushes, rose the main body of the wild men. With shouts of savage glee they leaped upon her. There was no chance for flight — in every direction brutal faces and murderous weapons barred her way.

With greater consideration than she had looked forward to they signaled her to accompany them. Stark was with them. To him slight humanity was shown. If he lagged, a spear point, already red with his blood, urged him to greater speed; but to the girl no cruelty nor indignity was shown.

In single file, the prisoners in the center of the column, the party made its way inland. All day they marched, until Stark, unused to this form of exertion, staggered and fell a dozen times each mile.

Nadara could almost have found it in her heart to be sorry for him, had it not been for the fact that she realized all too keenly that but for his own bestial brutality neither of them need have been there to be subjected to the present torture, and to be tortured by anticipation of horrors to come.

To the girl it seemed that her fate must be a thousand fold more terrible than the mere death the man was to suffer, for that these degraded savages would let him live seemed beyond the pale of reason. She pray to the God of which her Thandar had taught her for a quick and merciful death, yet while she prayed she well knew that no such boon could be expected.

She compared her captors to Korth and Flatfoot, with Big Fist and Thurg, nor did she look for greater compassion in them than in the men she had known best.

Late in the afternoon it became evident that Stark could proceed no farther unless the savages carried him. That they had any intention of so doing was soon disproved. The first officer of the *Priscilla* had fallen for the twentieth time. A dozen vicious spear thrusts failed to bring him staggering and tottering, to his feet as in the past.

The chief of the party approached the fallen white, kicking him in the sides and face, and at last pricking him with the sharp point of his parang. Stark but lay an inert mass of suffering flesh, and groaned. The chief grew angry. He grasped the white man around the body and raised him to his feet, but the moment that he released him Stark fell to the earth once more.

At last the warrior could evidently control his rage no further. With a savage whoop he swung his parang aloft, bringing it down full upon the neck of the prostrate white. The head, grinning horribly, rolled to Nadara's feet. She looked at it, lying there staring up at her out of its black and sightless eyes, without the slightest trace of emotion.

Nadara, the cave girl, was accustomed to death in all its most horrible and sudden forms. She saw before her but the head of an enemy. It was nothing to her — Stark had only himself to thank.

The chief gathered the severed head into a bit of bark cloth, and fastening it to the end of his spear, signaled his followers to resume the journey.

On and on they went, farther into the interior, and with them went Nadara, borne to what nameless fate she could but guess.

IX

BUILDING THE BOAT

*T*wo days after the earthquake that had saved Nadara from Thurg and wiped out the people of the girl's tribe, a man moved feebly beneath the tumbled debris from the foot top of is clogged cavern. It was Thandar. The tons of rock that had toppled from above and buried the entrance to this cave had passed him by unscathed, while the few pounds shaken from the ceiling had stunned him into a long enduring insensibility.

Slowly he regained consciousness, but it was a long time before he could marshal his faculties to even a slight appreciation of the catastrophe that had overwhelmed him. Then his first thought was of Nadara. He crawled to what had once been the entrance of his cave. He had not as yet linked the darkness to its real cause — he thought it was night. It had been night when he closed his eyes. How could he guess that

that had been three nights before, or all the cruel blows that fate had struck him since he slept?

At the opening from the cave he met his first surprise and setback — the way was blocked! What was the meaning of it? He tugged and pushed weakly upon the mass that barred him from escape. Who had imprisoned him? He recalled the vivid dream in which he had seen Nadara stolen away by Thurg. The recollection sent him frantically at the pile of shattered rock and loose debris which choked the doorway.

To his chagrin he found himself too weak to direct any long sustained effort against the obstacle. It occurred to him that he must have been injured. Whoever imprisoned him must first have beaten him. He felt of his head. Yes, there was a great gash, but his touch told him that it was not a new one. How long, then, had he been imprisoned? As he sat pondering this thing he became aware of the gnawing of hunger and the craving of thirst within his slowly awakening body. The sensations were almost painful. So much so that they forced him to a realization of the fact that he must have been without food or water for a considerable time.

Again he assailed the mass that held him prisoner, and as he burrowed slowly into it the truth dawned upon him. He recalled the rumblings of the Great Nagoola that had frightened Nadara the night of the council. A terrific quake had done this thing. Thandar shuddered as he thought of Nadara. Was she, too, imprisoned in her cave, or had the worst happened to her? Frantically now, he tore at the close-packed rubble. But he soon discovered that not in ill-directed haste lay his means of escape. Slowly and carefully, piece by piece, he must remove the broken rock until he had tunneled through to the outer world.

Reason told him that he was not deeply buried, for the fact that he lived and could breathe was sufficient proof that fresh air was finding its way through the debris, which it could not have done did the stuff lie before the cave in any considerable thickness.

Weak as he was he could work but slowly, so that it was several hours later before he caught the first glimpse of daylight beyond the obstacle. After that he progressed more rapidly, and presently he crawled through a small opening to view the wreckage of the shattered cliff.

A flock of vultures rose from their hideous feast as the sight of Thandar disturbed them. The man shuddered as he looked down upon the grisly things from which they had risen. Forgetting his hunger and his thirst he scrambled up over the tortured cliff face to where Nadara's cave had been. Its mouth was buried as his had been. Again he set to work, but this time is was easier. When at last he had opened a way within he hesitated for fear of the blighting sorrow that awaited him

At last, nerving himself to the ordeal, he crawled within the cave that had been Nadara's. Groping about in the darkness, expecting each moment to feel the body of his loved one cold in death, he at last covered the entire floor — there was no body within.

Hastily he made his way to the face of the cliff again, and then commenced a horrible and pitiful search among the ghastly remnants of men and women that lay scattered about among the tumbled rocks. But even here his search was vain, for the ghoulish scavengers had torn from their prey every shred of their former likenesses.

Weak, exhausted, sorrow ridden and broken, Thandar dragged himself painfully to the little river. Here he quenched his thirst and bathed his body. After, he sought food, and then he crawled to a hole he knew of in the riverbank, and curling up upon the dead grasses within, slept the sun around.

Refreshed and strengthened by his sleep and the food that he had taken, Thandar emerged from his dark warren with renewed hope. Nadara could not be dead! It as impossible. She must have escaped and be wandering about the island. He would search for her until he found her. But as day followed day and still no sign of Nadara, or any other living human being, he became painfully convinced that he alone of the inhabitants of the island had survived the cataclysm.

The thought of living on through a long life without her cast him into the blackest pit of despair. He reproached heaven for not having taken him as well, for without Nadara life was not worth living. With the passage of time his grief grew more rather than less acute. As it increased so too increased the horror of his loneliness. It island became a hated thing — life a mockery. The chances that a vessel would touch the shore again during his lifetime seemed remote indeed, unless his father sent out a relief party, but in his despair he did not even hope for such a contingency.

He would not take his own life, though the temptation was great, but he courted death in every form that the savage island owned. He slept out upon the ground at night. He sought Nagoola in his lair, and armed only with his light lance he leaped to close quarters with every one of the great cats he could find.

The wild boars, often as formidable as Nagoola himself, were hunted now as they never had been hunted before. Thandar lived high those days, and many were the panther pelts that lined his new-found cave in the cliff beside the sea — the same cliff in which Nadara had found shelter, and from whence she had gone away with the search party from the *Priscilla.*

One day as Thandar was returning from the beach where he often when to scan the horizon for a sail, he saw something moving at the foot of his cliff. Thandar dropped behind a bush, watching. A moment later the thing moved again, and Thandar saw that it was a man. Instantly he sprang to his feet and ran forward. The days that he had been without human companionship had seemed to drag themselves into as many weary months. Now he had reached the pinnacle of loneliness from which he would gladly have embraced the devil had he come in human guise.

Thandar ran noiselessly. He was almost upon the man, a great, hairy brute, before the fellow was aware of his presence. At first the fellow turned to run, but when he saw that Thandar was alone he remained to fight.

"I am Roof," he cried, "and I can kill you!"

The familiar primitive greeting no longer raised Thandar's temperature or filled him with the fire of battle. He wanted companionship now, not a quarrel.

"I am Thandar," he replied.

The slow-witted hulking brute recognized him, and stepped back a pace. He was not so keen to fight now that he had learned the identity of the man who faced him. He had seen Thandar in battle. He had witnessed Thurg's defeat at the hands of this smooth-skinned stranger.

"Let us not fight," continued Thandar. "We are alone upon the island. I have seen no other than you since the Great Nagoola came forth and destroyed the people. Let us be friends, hunting together in peace. Otherwise one of us must kill the other and thereafter live always alone until death releases him from his terrible solitude."

Roof peered over Thandar's shoulder toward the wood behind him.

"Are you alone?" he asked.

"Yes, have I not told you that all were killed but you and I?"

"All were not killed," replied Roof. "But I will be friends with Thandar. We will hunt together and cave together. Roof and Thandar are brothers."

He stooped, and gathering a handful of grass advanced toward the American. Thandar did likewise and when each had taken the peace offering of the other and rubbed it upon his forehead the ceremony of friendship was complete — simple but nonetheless effectual, for each knew that the other would rather die than disregard the primitive pact.

"You said all were not killed, Roof," said Thandar, the ceremony over. "What do you mean?"

"All were not killed by the Great Nagoola," replied the bad man. "Thurg was not killed, nor was she who was Thandar's mate — she whom Thurg would have stolen."

"What?" Thandar almost screamed the question. "Nadara is not dead?"

"Look," said Roof, and he led the way to the foot of the cliff. "See!"

"Yes," replied Thandar, "I had noticed that body, but what of it?"

"It was Thurg," explained Roof. "He sought to reach your mate, who had taken refuge in that cave far above us. Then came some strange men who made a great noise with sticks and Thurg fell dead — the loud noise had killed him from a great distance. Then came the strange men and she whom you call Nadara went away with them."

"In which direction?" cried Thandar. "Where did they take her?"

"They took her to the strange cliff in which they dwelt — the one in which they came. Never saw man such a thing as this cliff. It floated upon the face of the water. About its face were many tiny caves, but the people did not come out of these they came from the top of the cliff, and clambering down the sides floated ashore in hollow things of wood. On top of the cliff were two trees without leaves, and only very short upright branches. When the cliff went away black smoke came out of it from a short black stump of a tree between the two trees. It was a very wonderful thing to see; but the most wonderful of all were the noise-sticks that killed Thurg and Nagoola a long way off."

Not half of Roof's narrative did Thandar hear. Through his brain roared and thundered a single mighty thought: Nadara lives! Nadara lives! Life took on a new meaning to him now. He trembled at the thought of the chances he had been taking. Now, indeed, must he live. He leaped up and down, laughing and shouting. He threw his arms about the astonished Roof, whirling the troglodyte about in a mad waltz. Nadara lives! Nadara lives!

Once again the sun shone, the birds sag, nature was her old, happy, carefree shelf. Nadara was alive and among civilized men. But then came a doubt.

"Did Nadara go willingly with these strangers," he asked Roof, "or did they take her by force?"

"They did not take her by force," replied Roof. "They talked with her for a time, and then she took the hand of one of the men in hers, stroking it, and he placed his arm about her. Afterward they walked slowly to the edge of the great water where they got into the strange things that had brought them to the land, and returned to their floating cliff. Presently the smoke came out, as I have told you, and the cliff went away toward the edge of the world. But they are all dead now."

"What?" yelled Thandar.

"Yes, I saw the cliff since, very slowly when it was a long way off, until on the smoke was coming out of the water."

Thandar breathed a sigh of relief.

"Point," he said, "to the place where the cliff sank beneath the water."

Roof pointed almost due north.

"There," he said.

For days Thandar puzzled over the possible identity of the ship and the men with whom Nadara had gone so willingly. Doubtless some kindly mariner, hearing her story, had taken her home, away from the terrors and loneliness of this unhappy island. And now the man chafed to be after her, that he might search the world for his lost love.

To wait for a ship appeared quite impossible to the impatient Thandar, for he knew that a ship might never come. There was but one alternative, and had Waldo Emerson been a less impractical man in the world to which he had been born he would have cast aside that single alternative as entirely beyond the pale of possibility. But Waldo was only practical and wise in the savage ways of the primitive life to which circumstance had forced him to revert. And so he decided upon as fool-hardy and hair-brained a venture as the mind of man might conceive. It was no less a thing than to build a boat and set out upon the broad Pacific in search of a civilized port or a vessel that might bear him to such.

To Waldo it seemed quite practical. He realized of course that the venture would be fraught with peril, but would it not be better to die in an attempt to find his Nadara than to live on forever in the hopelessness of this forgotten island?

And so he set to work to build a boat. He had not tools but his crude knife and the razor the sailor of the *Sally Corwith* had given him, so it was quite impossible for him to construct a dugout. The possibilities that lie in fire did not occur to him. Finally he hit upon what seemed the only feasible form of construction.

With his knife he cut long, pliant saplings, and lesser branches. These he fashioned into a framework of a boat. Roof helped him, keenly interested in this new work. The ribs were fastened to the keel and gunwale by thongs of panther skin, and when the framework was completed panther skins were stretched over it. The edges of the skin were sewn together with threads of gut, as tightly as Thandar and Roof could pull them.

A mast was rigged well forward, and another panther skin from which the fur had been scrapped was fitted as a sail, square rigged. For rudder Thandar fashioned a long slender sapling, looped at one end, and the loop covered with skin laced tightly on. This he figured would serve as both rudder and paddle, as necessity demanded.

At last all was done. Together Thandar and Roof carried the light, crude skiff to the ocean. They waded out beyond the surf, and upon the crest of a receding swell they launched the thing, Thandar leaping in as it floated upon the water.

The sail was not taken along for this trial. Thandar merely wished to know that this craft would float, and right side up. For a moment it did so, until the sea rushing in at the loose seams filled it with water.

Thandar and Roof had great difficulty in dragging it out again upon the beach. Roof now would have given up, but not so Thandar. It is true that he was slightly disheartened, for he had set great store upon the success of his little vessel.

After they had carried the frail thing beyond high tide Thandar sat down upon the ground and for an hour he did naught but stare at the leaky craft. Then he arose and calling to Roof led him into the forest. For a mile they walked, and then Thandar halted before a tree from the side of which a thick and sticky stream was slowly oozing. Thandar had brought along a gourd, and now with a small branch he commenced transferring the mass from the side of the tree to the gourd. Roof helped him. In an hour the gourd was filled. Then they returned to the skiff.

Leaving the gourd there Thandar and Roof walked to a clump of heavy jungle grasses not far from the cliff where their cave lay. Here Thandar gathered a great armful of the yellow, ripened grass, telling Roof to do likewise. This they took back to the skiff, where, by rolling it assiduously between their hands and pounding it with stones they reduced it to a mass of soft, tough fiber.

Now Thandar showed Roof how to twist this fiber into a loose, fluffy rope, and when he had him well started he daubed the rope with the rubbery fluid he had filched from the tree, and with a sharp stick tucked it into every seam and crevice of the skiff.

It took the better part of two days to accomplish this, and when it was done and the gourd empty, the two men returned to the tree and refilled it. This time they built a fire upon their return to the skiff, Roof spinning a hardwood splinter rapidly between toes and fingers in a little mass of tinder that lay in a hollowed piece of wood. Presently a thin spiral of smoke arose from the tinder, growing denser for a moment until of a sudden it broke into flame.

The men piled twigs and branches upon the blaze until the fire was well started. Then Thandar taking a ball of the viscous matter from the gourd heated it in the flames, immediately daubing the melting mass upon the outside of the skiff. In this way, slowly and with infinite patience, the two at last succeeded in coating the entire outer surface of the canoe with a waterproof substance that might defy the action of water almost indefinitely.

For three days Thandar let the coating dry, and then the craft was given another trial. The man's heart was in his throat as the canoe floated upon the crest of a great wave and he leaped into it.

But a moment later he shouted in relief and delight — the thing floated like a cork, nor was there the slightest leak discernible. For half an hour Thandar paddled about the harbor, and then he returned for the sail. This too, though rather heavy and awkward, worked admirably, and the balance of the day he spent in sailing, even venturing out into the ocean.

Much of the time he paddled, for Waldo Emerson knew more of the galleys of ancient Greece than he did of sails or sailing, so that for the most part he sailed with the wind, paddling when he wished to travel in another direction. But, withal, his attempt filled him with delight, and he could scarce wait to be off toward civilization and Nadara.

The next two days were spent in collecting food and water, which Thandar packed in numerous gourds, sealing the mouths with the rubbery substance such as he had used to waterproof his craft. The flesh of the wild hog, and deer, and bird he cut in narrow strips and dried over a slow fire, in this work Roof assisted him, and at last all was in readiness for the venture.

The day of his departure dawned bright and clear. A gentle south wind gave promise of great speed toward the north. Thandar was wild with hope and excitement. Roof was to accompany him, but at the last moment the nerve of the troglodyte failed him, and he ran away and hid in the forest.

It was just as well, thought Thandar, for now his provisions would last twice as long. And so he set out upon his perilous adventure, braving the mighty Pacific in a frail and unseaworthy cockleshell with all the assurance and confidence that is ever born in ignorance.

X

THE HEADHUNTERS

*N*ature so far had been kind to Waldo Emerson Smith-Jones. No high winds or heavy seas had assailed him, and he had been upon the water for three days now. The wind had held steadily out of the south, varying but a few points during this time but even so Waldo Emerson was commencing to doubt and to worry. His supply of water was running dangerously low, his food supply would last but a few days longer; and as yet he had sighted no sail, nor seen any land. Furthermore, he had not the remotest conception of how he might retrace his way to the island he had just quitted. He could only sail before the wind. Should the wind veer around into the north he might, by chance, be blown back to the island. Otherwise he never could reach it. And he was beginning to wonder if he had not been a trifle too precipitate in his abandonment of land.

In common with most other landsmen, Waldo Emerson had little conception of the vastness of the broad reaches of unbroken water wildernesses that roll in desolate immensity over three quarters of the globe. His recollection of maps pictured the calm and level sea dotted, especially in the south seas, with many islands. Their names, often, were quite reassuring. He recollected, among others, such as the Society Islands, the Friendly Islands, and Christmas Island. He hoped that he would land upon one of these. There were so many islands upon the maps, and they seemed so close together that he was not a little mystified that he had failed to sight several hundred before this.

And ships! It appeared incredible that he should have seen not a single sail. He distinctly recalled the atlas he had examined prior to embarking upon his health cruise. The Pacific had been lined in all directions with routes of long established steamer lanes, and in between, Waldo had felt, the ocean must be dotted with innumerable tramps that come and go between the countless ports that fringe the major sea.

And yet for three days nothing had broken the dull monotony of the vast circle of which he was always the center and the sole occupant. In three days, thought Waldo, he must have covered an immense distance.

And three more days dragged their weary lengths. The wind had died to the faintest of breezes. The canoe was just making headway and that was all. The water was gone. The food nearly so. Waldo was suffering from lack of the former. The pitiless sun beating down upon him increased his agony. He stretched his panther skin across the stern and hid beneath it from the torrid rays. And there he lay until darkness brought relief.

During the night the wind sprang up again, but this time from the west. It rose and with it rose the sea. The man, clinging to his crude steering plank, struggled to keep the light craft straight before the wind which was now howling fearfully while great waves, hungry and wide jawed, raced after him like a pack of ravenous wolves.

Thandar knew that the unequal struggle against the mighty forces of the elements could not endure for long. It seemed that each fierce gust of brutal wind must tear his frail boat to shreds, and yet it was the very lightness of the thing that saved it, for it rode upon the crests of the waves, blown forward at terrific velocity like a feather before the hurricane.

In Thandar's heart was no terror — only regret that he might never again see his mother, his father, or his Nadara. Yet the night wore on and still he fled before the storm. The sky was overcast — the darkness was impenetrable. He imagined all about him still the same wide, tenantless circle of water, only now storm-torn and perpendicular and black, instead of peacefully horizontal, and soothingly blue-green. And then, even as he was thinking about this, there rose before him a thunderous booming loud above the frenzied bedlam of the storm. His boat was lifted high in the air to dive headforemost into what might be a bottomless abyss for all Thandar knew. But it was not bottomless. The canoe struck something and stopped suddenly, pitching Thandar into a boiling maelstrom. A great wave picked him up, carrying with race-horse velocity within its crest. He felt himself hurled pitilessly upon smooth, hard sand. The water tried to drag him back, but he fought with toes and fingers, clutching at the surface of the stuff upon which he had been dropped. Then the wave abandoned him and raced swiftly back into the sea.

Thandar was exhausted, but he knew that he must crawl up out of the way of the surf, or be dragged back by the next roller. What he had searched for in vain through six long days he had run down in the midst of a Stygian night. He had found land! Or, to be more explicit, land had got in front of him and he had run into it. He had commenced to wonder if some terrible convulsions of nature had not swallowed up all the land in the world, leaving only a waste of desolate water. He forgot his hunger and his thirst in the happiness of the knowledge that once more he was upon land. He wondered a little what land it might be. He hoped that dawn would reveal the chimneys and steeples of a nearby city. And then, exhausted, he fell into a deep sleep.

It was the sun shining down into his upturned face that awoke him. He was lying upon his back beside a clump of bushes a little way above the beach. He was about to rise and survey the new world into which fate and a hurricane had hurled him, when he heard a familiar sound upon the opposite side of his bush. It was the movement of an animal creeping through the long grass.

Thandar, the caveman, came noiselessly to his hands and knees, peering cautiously through the intervening network of branches. What he saw sent his hand groping for his wooden sword with its fire-hardened point. There, not five paces from him, was a man going cautiously upon all fours. It was the most horrible appearing man that Thandar had ever seen — even Thurg appeared lovely by comparison. The creature's ears were split and heavy ornaments had dragged them down until the lobes rested upon its shoulders. The face was terribly marked with cicatrices and tattooing. The teeth were black and pointed. A headdress of long feathers waved and nodded above the hideous face. There was much tattooing upon the arms and legs and abdomen; the breasts were circled with it. In a belt about the waist lay a sword in its scabbard. In the man's hand was a long spear.

The warrior was creeping stealthily upon something at Thandar's left. The latter looked in the direction the other's savage gaze was bent. Through the bushes he could barely discern a figure moving toward them along the edge of the beach. The warrior had passed him now and Thandar stood erect the better to obtain a view of the fellow's quarry.

Now he saw it plainly — a man strangely garbed in many colors. A yellow jacket, soiled and worn, covered the upper part of his body. Strange designs, very elaborate, were embroidered upon the garment which reached barely to the fellow's waist. Beneath was a red sash in which were stuck a long pistol and a wicked-looking knife. Baggy blue trousers reached to the bare ankles and feet. A strip of crimson cloth wound around the head completed the strange garmenture. The features of the man were Mongolian.

Thandar could see the warrior pause as it became evident that the other was approaching directly toward his place of concealment, but at the last moment the unconscious quarry turned sharply to his right down upon the beach. He had discovered the wreck of Thandar's canoe and was going to investigate it.

The move placed Thandar almost between the two. Suddenly the native rose to his feet — his victim's back was toward him. Grasping his spear in his left hand he drew his wicked-looking sword and emerged cautiously from the bushes. At the same moment the man upon the beach wheeled quickly as though suddenly warned of his danger. The native, discovered, leaped forward with raised sword. The man snatched his pistol from his belt, leveled it at the on-rushing warrior and pulled the trigger. There was a futile click — that was all. The weapon had missed fire.

Instantly, a third element was projected into the fray. Thandar, seeing a more direct link to civilization in the strangely appareled Mongol than in the naked savage, leaped to the assistance of the former. With drawn sword he rushed out upon the savage. The wild man turned at Thandar's cry, which he had given to divert the fellow's attention from his now almost helpless victim.

Thandar knew nothing of the finer points of swordplay. He was ignorant of the wickedness of a Malay parang — the keen, curved sword of the headhunter, so he rushed in upon the savage has he would have upon one of Thurg's near-men.

The very impetuosity of his attack awed the native. For a moment he stood his ground, and then, with a cry of terror turned to flee; but he had failed to turn soon enough. Thandar was upon him. The sharp point entered his back beneath the left shoulder black, and behind it were the weight and sinews of the caveman. With a shriek the savage lunged forward, clutching at the cruel point that now protruded from his breast. When he touched the earth he was dead.

Thandar drew his sword from the body of the headhunter and turned toward the man he had rescued. The latter was approaching, taking excitedly. It was evident that he was thanking Thandar, but no word of his strange tongue could the American understand. Thandar shook his head to indicate that he was unfamiliar with the other's language, and then the latter dropped into pidgin English, which, while almost as unintelligible to the cultured Bostonian, still contained the battered remnants of some few words with which he was familiar.

Thandar depreciated his act by means of gestures, immediately following these with signs to indicate he was hungry and thirty. The stranger evidently understood him, for he motioned for him to follow, leading the way back along the beach in the direction from which he had come.

Before starting, however, he had pointed to the wreck of Thandar's canoe and then toward Thandar, nodding his head questioningly as to ask if the boat belonged to the caveman.

Around the end of the promontory they came upon a little cove beside the beach of which Thandar saw a camp of nearly a score of men similar in appearance to his guide. These were preparing breakfast beside the partially completed hull of a rather large boat they seemed to have been building.

At sight of Thandar they looked their astonishment, but after hearing the story of their fellow they greeted the caveman warmly, furnishing him with food and water in abundance.

For three days Thandar worked with these men upon their craft, picking up their story slowly with a slow acquirement of a bowing acquaintance with the bastard tongue they used when speaking with him. He soon became aware of the fact that fate had thrown him among a band of pirates. There were Chinese, Japanese, and Malays among them — the offscourings of the south seas; men who had become discredited even among the villainous pirates of their own lands, and had been forced to join their lots in this remoter and less lucrative field, under an unhung ruffian, Tsao Ming, the Chinaman whose life Thandar had saved.

He also learned that the storm that had cast them upon this shore nearly a month before had demolished their prahu, and what with the building of another and numerous skirmishes with the savages they had had a busy time of it.

Only yesterday while a part of them had been hunting a mile or two inland they had been attacked by savages who had killed two and captured one of their number.

They told Thandar that these savages were the most ferocious of headhunters, but like the majority of their kind preferred ambushing an unwary victim to meeting him in fair fight in the open. Thandar did not doubt but that the latter mode of warfare would have been entirely to the liking of his piratical friends, for never in his life had he dreamed, even, of so ferocious and warlike a band as was comprised in this villainous and bloodthirsty aggregation. But the constant

nervous tension under which they had worked, never knowing at what instant an arrow or lance would leap from the
shades of the jungle to pierce them in the back, had reduced
them to a state of fear that only a speedy departure from the
island could conquer.

Their boat was almost completed, two more days would
see them safely launched upon the ocean, and Taso Ming had
promised Thandar that he would carry him to a civilized port
from which he could take a steamer on his return to America.

Late in the afternoon of the third day since his arrival
among the pirates, the men were suddenly startled by the
appearance of an exhausted and blood smeared apparition
amongst them. From the nearby jungle the man had staggered
to fall halfway across the clearing, spent.

It was Boloon — he who had been captured by the headhunters the day before Thandar had been cast upon the shore.
Revived with food and water the fellow told a most extraor-
dinary tale. Even from the meager scraps that were afterward
translated into pidgin English for Thandar the Bostonian
learned the Boloon had been dragged far inland to a village
of considerable size.

Here he had been placed in a room of one of the long
houses to await the pleasure of the chief. It was hinted that
he was to be tortured before his head was removed to grace
the rafters of the chief's palace.

The remarkable portion of his tale related to a strange
temple to which he had been dragged and thrown at the feet
of a white goddess. Tsao Ming and the other pirates were
much mystified by this part of the story, for Boloon insisted
that the goddess was white with a mass of black hair, and that
her body was covered in the pelt of a magnificent black
panther.

Though Taso Ming pointed out that there were no panthers
upon this island Boloon could not be shaken. He had seen
with his own eyes, and he knew. Furthermore, he argued, there
were no white goddesses upon the island, and yet the woman
he had seen was white.

When this strange tale was retold to Thandar he could not
but recall that Nadara had worn a black panther skin, but of
course it could not be Nadara — that was impossible. But yet

he asked for a further description of the goddess — the color of her eyes and hair — the proportions of her body — her height.

To all these questions Boloon gave replies that but caused Thandar's excitement to wax stronger. And then came the final statement that set him in a frenzy of hope and apprehension.

"Upon her left hand was a great diamond," said Boloon.

Thandar turned toward Tsao Ming.

"I go inland to the temple," he said, "to see who this white goddess may be. If you wait two days for me and I return you shall have as much gold as you ask in payment. If you do not wait repair my canoe and hide it in the bushes where the man hid who would have killed you but for Thandar."

"I shall wait three days," replied Tsao Ming. "Nor will I take a single *fun* in pay. You saved the life of Tsao Ming — that is not soon to be forgotten. I would send men with you, but they would not go. They are afraid of the headhunters. Too, will I repair your canoe against your coming after the third day; but," and he shrugged, "you will not come upon the third day, nor upon the fourth, nor ever, Thandar. It is better that you forget the foolish story of the frightened Boloon and come away from the accursed land with Tsao Ming."

But Thandar would not relinquish his intention, and so he parted with the pirates after receiving from Boloon explicit directions for his journey toward the mysterious temple and the white goddess who might be Nadara; and yet who could not be.

Straight into the tangled jungle he plunged, carrying the spear and parang of the headhunter he had killed, and in the string about his loins one of the long pistols of a dead pirate. This latter Tsao Ming had forced upon him with a supply of ammunition.

XI

THE RESCUE

It was dusk of the second day when Thandar, following the directions given him by Boloon, came to the edge of the little clearing within which rose the dingy outlines of many long houses raised upon piles. Before the village ran a river. Many times had Thandar crossed and recrossed this stream, for he had become lost twice upon the way and had to return part way each time to pick up his trail.

In the center of the village the man could see the outlines of a loftier structure rearing its head above those of the others. As darkness fell Thandar crept closer toward his goal — the large building which Boloon had described as the temple.

Beneath the high raised houses the caveman crept, disturbing pigs and chickens as he went, but their noise was no uncommon thing, and rather than being a menace to his safety it safeguarded him, for it hid the noise of his own advance.

At last he came beneath a house nearest the temple. The moon was full and high. Her brilliant light flooded the open spaces between the buildings, casing into black darkness the shadows beneath. In one of these Thandar lurked. He saw that the temple was guarded. Before its only entrance squatted two warriors. How was he to pass them?

He moved to the end of the shadow of the house beneath which he spied as far from the guards as possible; but still discovery seemed certain were he to attempt to rush across the intervening space. He was at a loss as to what next to do. It seemed foolish to risk all now upon a bold advance — the time for such a risk would be when he had found the goddess and learned if she were Nadara, or another; but how might he cross that strip of moonlight and enter the temple past the two guards without risk?

He moved silently to the far end of the building, in the shadows of which he watched. For some time he stood looking across at his goal, so near, and yet seemingly infinitely further from attainment than the day he had left the coast in search of it. He noted the long poles stuck into the ground at irregular intervals about the structure. He wondered at the significance of the rude carving upon them, of the barbaric capitals sometimes topped by the headdress of a savage warrior, again by a dried and grinning skull, or perhaps the rudely chiseled likeness of a hideous human face.

Upon many of the poles were hung shields, weapons, clothing and earthenware vessels. One especially was so weighted down by its heterogeneous burden that it leaned drunkenly against the eaves of the temple. Thandar's eye followed it upward to where it touched the crudely shingled roof. The suggestion was sufficient — where his eye had climbed he would climb. There as only the moonlight to make the attempt perilous. If the clouds would but come! But there was no indication of clouds in the star-shot sky.

He looked toward the guards. They lolled at the opposite end of the temple, only one of them being visible. The other was hidden by the angle of the building. The back of the fellow whom Thandar could see was turned toward the caveman. If they remained thus for a moment he could reach the roof unnoticed. But then there was the danger of discovery from one of the other buildings. An occasional whiff of tobacco smoke told him that some of the men were still awake upon the verandahs where most of the youths and bachelors slept.

Thandar crawled to where he could see the only verandah which directly faced the portion of the temple he had chosen for his attempted entrance. For an hour he watched the rising and falling glow of the cigarettes of two of the native men, and listened to the low hum of their conversation. The hour seemed to drag into an eternity, but at last the glowing butt of first one cigarette and then another was flicked over into the grass and silence reigned upon the verandah.

For half an hour longer Thandar waited. The guards before the temple still squatted as before. The one Thandar could see seemed to have fallen asleep, for his head drooped forward upon his breast.

The time had come. There was no need of further delay or reconnaissance — if he was to be discovered that would be the end of it, and it would not profit him one iota to know a second or so in advance of the alarm that he had been detected. So he did not waste time in stealthy advance, or in much looking this way and that. Instead he moved swiftly, though silently, directly across the open, moonlit space to the foot of the leaning pole. He did not cast a glance behind nor to the right nor left. His whole attention was riveted upon the thing in hand.

Thandar had scaled the rickety, toppling saplings of the cliff dweller for so long that this pole offered no greater difficulties to him than would an ordinary staircase to you or me. First he tested it with eyes and hands to know that it rested securely at the top and that beneath his weight it would not move noisily out of its present position.

Assured that it seemed secure, Thandar ran up it with the noiseless celerity of a cat. Gingerly he stepped upon the roof, not knowing the manner of its construction, which might be weak thatching that would give beneath him and precipitate him into the interior beneath.

To his surprise and consternation he found that the roof was of wood, and quite as solid as one could imagine. It had been his plan to enter the temple from above, but now it seemed that he was to be thwarted, for he could not hope to cut silently through a wooden roof with his parang in the few hours that intervened before dawn.

He stooped to examine the roof minutely with eyes and fingers. The moonlight was brilliant. In it he could see quite well. He pulled away the thin palm-frond thatch. Beneath were shingles hand-hewn from billian. In each was a small square black hole through which passed a strip of rattan that bound the shingle to the frame of the roof.

Thandar lifted away the thatching over a little space some two feet square. Then he inserted the point of his keen parang beneath a rattan tie string, and an instant later had lifted aside a shingle. Another and another followed the first until and opening in the roof had been made large enough to easily admit his body.

Thandar leaned over and peered into the darkness beneath. He could see nothing. His own body was between the moon and the hole in the roof, shutting out the rays of the satellite from the interior.

The man lowered his legs cautiously over the edge of the hole. Feeling about, his feet came in contact with a rafter. A moment later his whole body had disappeared with the temple. Clinging to the edge of the hold with one hand, Thandar squatted upon the rafter above the temple floor.

Now that his body no longer closed the aperture in the roof the moonlight poured through it throwing a brilliant flood upon a portion of the floor at the opposite side of the interior. The balance was feebly lighted by the diffused moon-light.

The temple seemed to consist of a single large room. In the center was a raised platform, and also about the walls. From the rafters hung baskets containing human skulls — one sung directly in the moonlight beneath Thandar. He could see its grisly contents plainly.

His eyes followed the moonlight toward the area which it touched upon the far side of the room. It reminded Waldo Emerson of a spot light thrown from the gallery of theater upon the stage.

Directly in the center of the light a woman lay asleep upon the platform. Thandar's heart stood still. About her figure was wrapped the glossy hide of Nagoola. Over one bare, brown arm spilled a wealth of thick, black hair, fine as silk, upon the third finger of the left hand blazed a large solitaire. The woman's face was turned toward the wall — but Thandar knew that he could not be mistaken — it was Nadara.

From the rafter upon which he squatted to the floor below was not over twelve or fifteen feet. Thandar swung downward, clinging to the rafter with his hands, and dropped, catlike, upon his naked feet to the floor below.

The almost noiseless descent was sufficient, however, to awaken the sleeper. With the quickness of a panther she swung around and was upon her feet facing the man almost the instant he alighted. The moonlight was now full upon her face. Thandar rushed forward to take her in his arms.

"Nadara!" he whispered. "Thank God!"

The girl shrank back. She recognized the voice and the figure; but — her Thandar was dead! How could it be that he had returned from death? She was frightened.

The man saw the evident terror of her action, and paused.

"What is the matter, Nadara?" he asked. "Don't you know me? Don't you know Thandar?"

"Thandar is dead," she whispered.

The man laughed. In a few words he explained that he had been stunned, but not killed, by the earthquake. Then he came to her side and took her in his arms.

"Do I feel like a dead man?" he asked.

She put her arms about his neck and drew his face down to hers. She was sobbing. Thandar's back was toward the doorway of the temple. Nadara was facing it. As she raised her eyes to his again her face when deadly white, and she dragged and pushed him suddenly out of the brilliant patch of moonlight.

"The guard!" she whispered. "I just saw something move beyond the door."

Thandar stepped behind one of the tree trunks that supported the roof, looking toward the entrance. Yes, there was a man even now coming into the temple. His eyes were wide with surprise as he glanced upward to the hold in the roof. Then he looked in the direction of the platform upon which Nadara had been sleeping. When he saw that it was empty he ran back to the doorway and called his companion.

As he did so Thandar grasped Nadara's hand and drew her around the opposite side of the temple where the shadows were blackest, toward the doorway. They had reached the end of the room when the two warriors came running in, jabbering excitedly. One of them had passed halfway across the temple, and Thandar and Nadara had almost reached the door when the second savage caught sight of them. With a cry of warning to his companion he turned upon them with drawn parang.

As the fellow rushed forward Thandar drew the pistol the pirates had given him and fired point blank at the fellow's breast. With a howl the man staggered back and collapsed upon the floor. Then his fellow rushed to the attack.

Thandar had no time to reload. He handed the weapon to Nadara.

"In the pouch at my right side are cartridges," he said. "Get out several of them, and when I can I will reload."

As he spoke they had been edging toward the doorway. From the street beyond they could already hear excited voices raised in questioning. The shot had aroused the village.

Now the fellow with the parang was upon them. Thandar was clumsy with the unaccustomed weapon with which he tried to meet the attack of the skilled savage. There could have been but one outcome of the unequal struggle had not Nadara, always quick-witted and resourceful, snatched a long spear from the temple wall.

As she dragged it down there fell with it a clattering skull that broke upon the floor between the fighters. A howl of dismay and rage broke from the lips of the headhunter. This was sacrilege. The holy of the holies had been profaned. With renewed ferocity he leaped to close quarters with Thandar, but at the same instant Nadara lunged the sharp pointed spear into his side, his guard dropped and Thandar's parang fell full upon his skull.

"Come!" cried Nadara. "Make your escape the way you came. There is no hope for you if you remain. I will tell them that the two guards fought between themselves for me — that one killed the other, and that I shot the victor to save myself. They will believe me — I will tell them that I have always had the pistol hidden beneath my robe. Good-bye, my Thandar. We cannot both escape. If you will remain we may both die — you certainly."

Thandar shook his head vehemently.

"We shall both go — or both die," he replied.

Nadara pressed his hand.

"I am glad," was all she said.

The savages were pouring from their long houses. The street before the temple was filling with them. To attempt to escape in that direction would have been but suicidal.

"Is there no other exit?" asked Thandar.

"There is a small window in the back of the temple," replied Nadara, "in a little room that is sometimes used as a prison for those who are to die, but it lets out into another street which by this time is probably filled with natives."

"There is the floor," cried Thandar. "We will try the floor there."

He ran to the main entrance to the temple and closed the doors. Then he dragged the two corpses before them. And a long wooden bench. There was no other movable thing in the temple that had any considerable weight.

This done he took Nadara's hand and together the two ran for the little room. Here again they barricaded the door, and Thandar turned toward the floor. With his parang he pried up a board — it was laid but roughly upon the light logs that were the beams. Another was removed with equal ease, and then he lowered Nadara to the ground beneath the temple.

Clinging to the piling, Thandar replaced the boards above his head before he, too, dropped to the ground at Nadara's side. The streets upon either side of the temple were filled with savages. They could hear them congregating before the entrance to the temple where all was now quite and still within. They were bolstering their courage by much shouting to the point that would permit them to enter and investigate. They called the names of the guards, but there was no response.

"Give me the pistol," said Thandar.

He loaded it, keeping several cartridges ready in his hand. Then, with Nadara at his side, he crept to the back of the temple. Pigs, routed form their slumbers, grunted and complained. A dog growled at them. Thandar silenced it with a cut from his parang. When they reached the edge of the shadow beneath the temple they saw that there were only a few natives upon this side of the structure, and they were hurrying rapidly toward the front of the building. A hundred yards away was the jungle.

Now a sudden quiet fell upon the horde before the temple doors. There was the sound of hammering, then a pushing, scraping noise, and presently shouts of savage rage — the dead bodies of the guardsmen had been discovered. Now, from above, came the padding of naked feet running through the temple. The street behind was momentarily deserted.

"Now!" whispered Thandar.

He seized Nadara's hand, and together the two raced from beneath the temple out into the moonlight and across the intervening space between the long houses toward the jungle. Halfway across, a belated native, emerging from the verandah of a nearby house, saw them. He set up a terrific yell and dashed toward them.

Thandar's pistol roared, and the savage dropped; but the signal had been given and before the two reached the jungle a screaming horde of warrior was upon their heels.

Thandar was confused. He had lost his bearings since entering the village and the temple. He turned toward Nadara.

"I do not know the way to the coast," he cried.

The girl took his hand.

"Follow me," she said, and to the memories of each leaped the recollection of the night she had led hem through the forest from the cliffs of the bad men. Once again was Waldo Emerson Smith-Jones, the learned, indebted to the greater wisdom of the unlettered cave girl for his salvation.

Unerringly Nadara ran through the tangled jungle in the direction of the coast. Though she had been but once over the way, she followed the direct line as unerringly as though each tree was blazed and sign posts marked each turn.

Behind them came the noise of the pursuit, but always Nadara and Thandar fled ahead of it. Not once did it gain upon them during the long hours of flight.

It was noon before they reached the coast. They came out at the camp of the pirates, but to Thandar's dismay it was deserted. Tsao Ming had awaited the allotted time and gone. If Thandar had but known it, the picturesque cutthroat had overstayed the promised period, and had but scarce left when the fugitives had emerged from the jungle beside the beach. In fact his rude craft was but out of sight beyond the northern promontory. A pistol shot would have recalled him; but Thandar did not know it, and so he turned dejectedly to search for his hidden canoe.

It lay behind the little clump of bushes that had hidden Thandar the morning that he had saved Tsao Ming's life, several hundred yards to the south.

All signs of pursuit had now ceased, and so the two walked slowly in the direction of the craft. They found it just where Tsao Ming had promised that it would be. It was well and staunchly repaired, and in addition contained a goodly supply of food and water. Thandar blessed Tsao Ming, the unhung murderer.

Together they dragged the frail thing to the water's edge, and were about to shove it out when, with a chorus of savage yells, a score or more of the headhunters leaped from the jungle and bore down upon them. Thandar turned to meet them with drawn pistol.

"Get the canoe into the water, Nadara," he called to the girl. "I will hold them off until it is launched, then we may be able to reach deep water before they can overtake us."

Nadara struggled with the unwieldy boat which the rollers picked up and hurled back upon her each time she essayed to launch it. From the corner of his eyes Thandar saw the difficulties that the girl was having. Already the horde was halfway across the beach, running rapidly toward them. The man feared to fire except at close range since his unfamiliarity with firearms rendered him and extremely poor shot. However, it was evident that Nadara could not launch the thing alone, and so Thandar turned his pistol upon the approaching savages, pulled the trigger, and wheeled to assist the girl.

More by chance than skill the bullet lodged in the body of the foremost headhunter. The fellow rolled screaming to the sand, and as one his companions came to a sudden halt. But seeing that Thandar was busy with the boat and not appearing to intend to follow up his shot they presently resumed the charge.

Thandar and Nadara were having all that they could attend to with the canoe and so the savages came to the water's edge before they realized their proximity. When he saw them, Thandar wheeled and fired again, then picking the canoe up bodily above his head he struggled out through the surf, Nadara walking by his side, steadying him.

After them came the savages — perhaps half a dozen of the bolder, when suddenly a great roller caught them all, pursuers and pursued, sweeping them out into deep water. Thandar and Nadara clung to the canoe, but the headhunters were dragged down by the undertow.

Upon the beach, yelling, threatening and gesticulating, danced thirty or forty baffled savages; but now Thandar and Nadara had crawled into the craft, which the outgoing tide was carrying rapidly from shore, and with the aid of the paddle were soon safely out upon the bosom of the Pacific.

Safely?

XII

PIRATES

*A*s the tide and wind carried the light craft out to sea, and the shore line sank beneath the horizon behind them, Waldo Emerson looked out upon the future as he did upon the tumbling waste of desolate water encircling them, with utter hopelessness.

Once before he had passed by a miracle through the many-sided menaces of the sea; but that he should be so fortunate again he could not hope. And now Nadara was with him. Before, only his suffering and death had been possible; now he must face the greater agony of witnessing Nadara's.

The wind, blowing a steady gale, was raising a considerable sea. The vast billows rolled, one upon the heels of another, with the regularity of infantry units doubling at review. The wind and the sea seemed to have been made to order for the frail vessel that bore Thandar and Nadara. It rode the long, ponderous waves like a cork; its crude sail caught the wind and bellied bravely to it, driving the boat swiftly over the water.

And scarce had the shore behind them sunk forever from their sight than dead ahead another shoreline showed. Thandar could scarce believe his eyes. He rubbed them and looked again. Then he asked Nadara to look.

"What is that ahead?" he asked.

The girl half rose with an exclamation of joy.

"Land!" she cried.

And land it was. The wind, driving them madly, carried them toward the north end of what appeared to be a large island. Angry breakers pounded a rocky coast line. To strike there would mean instant death to them both. But would they strike? As they neared the point of the island it became evident to Thandar that they would be borne past it. Could he hope to stem the speed of the little craft and turn it back into the sheltered water in the lee of the land? The chances were more than even that the canoe would capsize the instant he cut away the sail and attempted to paddle across the wind; as would be necessary to come about the end of the island.

But there seemed no other way. He handed his parang to Nadara, telling her to be ready to cut the rawhide strips that supported the sail the instant that he gave the word. With his paddle clutched tightly in his hands he knelt in the stern, watching the progress of the canoe past the rocky point.

At this extremity of the island a narrow tongue of land ran far out into the sea. It as past the outer point of this tongue that the canoe was racing. When they had passed Thandar realized the rashness of attempting to turn the canoe into the trough of the sea even for the little distance that would have been necessary to make the shelter of the point, where, almost within reach, he could see the peaceful bosom of unruffled water lying safely behind the island.

And yet as he looked ahead upon the limitless waste of ocean before them he knew that one risk was not greater than the other, and then an alternative plan occurred to him. He would run a short distance past the point and then turn almost directly back and attempt the paddle the canoe in the calm water running nearly into the face of the wind, thus avoiding the dangers of the trough.

There was but a single drawback to this plan — the question of his ability to drive the canoe against the gale. At least it was worth trying. He gave Nadara the word to cut down the sail, and at the same instant, the canoe being upon the crest of a wave, he bent to the paddle. As the panther skin tumbled at the foot of the rough mast the nose of the craft swung around in reply to Thandar's vigorous strokes.

So intent were both upon the life and death struggle that they were waging with the elements that neither saw the long, low-lying craft that shot from the mouth of a small harbor behind them as they came into view upon the lee side of the island.

For a moment the canoe hung broadside to the wind. Thandar struggled frantically to carry it about. Down they dropped into the trough of a great sea. Above them hung the overleaning tower of the wave's crest ready to topple upon them its tons of water. The canoe rose, still broadside, almost to the crest of the wave — then the thing broke upon them.

When Thandar came to the surface his first thought was for Nadara. He looked about as he shook the water from his eyes. Almost at his side Nadara's head rose from the sea. As her eyes met his a smile touched her lips.

"This is better," she shouted. "Now we can reach the shore," and turning she struck out for land.

Just behind her swam Thandar. He knew that Nadara was like a fish in water, but he doubted her ability as he doubted his own to reach the shore in the face of both wind and tide. A wave carried them high in air, and from its crest both saw simultaneously a long craft in the hollow beneath them, and noted the fierce aspect of her crew.

Nadara, fearing all men but Thandar, would have attempted to elude the craft, but the glimpse that the man had of those aboard her convinced him that he had fallen by good fortune into the company of Tsao Ming and his crew.

"They are friends," he screamed to Nadara, and so they let the boat come alongside and pick them up; but no sooner had Thandar obtained a good look at the occupants that he discovered that never a face among them had he seen before.

They were men of the same type as Tsao Ming's motley horde, nor did Waldo Emerson need inquire their vocation — thief and murderer were writ upon every countenance. They jabbered questions at Nadara and Thandar in an assortment of dialects which neither could understand, and it was only after the craft had been anchored into the little bay and the party had waded to shore that Thandar tried speaking with them in pidgin English. Several among them understood him, and he was not long in making it plain to them that they would be paid well if they carried him and Nadara to a civilized port.

The leader, who seemed to be a full blooded Negro, laughed at him, ridiculing the idea that an almost naked man could pay for his liberty. At the same time the fellow cast such greedy glances at Nadara that Thandar became convinced that the fellow, for reasons of his own, preferred not to believe that they could pay in money for their liberty.

It seemed that the party had been about to embark for another portion of the western coast of the island where the main body of the horde lay. They had but been waiting for three of their crew who had gone inland hunting, when they had seen the canoe and put out to capture its occupants. Now they returned to the little harbor to pick up their fellows and continue toward the main camp.

The black was for dispatching Thandar at once as their boat was already overcrowded, but there were others who counseled him against it, reminding him of the probably anger of their chief, who saw only in a dead prisoner the loss of a possible ransom.

At last the hunters returned and all embarked. Soon the boat had passed out of the bay and was making its way south along the west coast of the island. It was almost dark when her nose was turned toward shore and the long sweeps brought into play as the sail sagged to the foot of the mast.

Between two small, overlapping points that hid what lay behind, they passed into a landlocked harbor. As the boat breasted the end of the inner point, Thandar sprang to his feet with a cry of joy and amazement. Now a hundred yards away, riding quietly on the mirrorlike surface of the water, lay the *Priscilla.*

The pirates looked at their prisoner in astonishment. The black rose with clenched fists as though prepared to strike him.

"*Priscilla* ahoy!" shrieked Waldo Emerson. "Help! Help!"

The Negro grinned. There was no response from the white yacht. Then the men told Thandar that they had captured the vessel several weeks before, and were holding her crew prisoners upon land awaiting the return of the chief who had been unaccountably absent for a long time. When Waldo Emerson told them that the yacht belong to his father the black was glad that he had not killed him, for he should bring a fat ransom.

It was dark when they landed, and Thandar and Nadara were forced into the squalid huts that lay side by side with several others just above the beach. For a long time the man could not sleep. His mind was occupied with doubts as to the fate of his father and mother. Nadara had told him that both had been aboard the *Priscilla.* She had said nothing of the treatment accorded her by Mrs. Smith-Jones, but Waldo had guess near the truth, and he had seen that the sight of the *Priscilla* had awakened not enthusiasm or happiness in the girl.

After awhile he dozed only to be awakened by the sound of movement outside his hut. There was something sinister in the stealthiness of the sound. Silently Thandar rose and crept to the door. The pirates had made no attempt to secure their prisoners — there was no possibility of their escaping from the island.

Thandar put his head out into the lesser darkness of the night. He muttered a little growl of rage and fear, for what he saw was the huge, dark bulk of a man crawling into Nadara's hut. Instantly the American followed. At the door of the girl's shelter he paused to listen. Within he heard a sudden exclamation of fright and the sound of a scuffle. Then he was within the darkness, and a moment later stumbled against a man. Thandar's fingers sought the throat. He made no sound. The other wheeled upon him with a knife. Thandar had expected it. His forearm warded the first blow, and

running down the forearm of the other found the knife wrist.
Then commenced the struggle within the Stygian blackness
of the interior of the hut. Back and forth across the mud
floor the two staggered and reeled — the one attempting to
wrench free the hand that held the knife — the other seeking
a hold upon the throat of his antagonist while he strode to
maintain his grip on the other's wrist. The heavy breathing
of the two rose and fell upon the silence of the night — that
and the scuffling of their feet were the only sounds of combat.
Nadara could not assist Thandar — she knew that it was he
who had come to her rescue though she could not see him.

At last, with superhuman effort, the night prowler broke
away from Thandar. For a moment silence reigned in the hut.
None of the three could see the other. From beneath his
panther skin Thandar drew the long pistol that Tsao Ming
had given him, but he dared not fire for fear of hitting
Nadara, nor dared he ask her to speak that he might know
her position, for them he would have divulged his own to
his antagonist.

For minutes that seemed like hours the three stood in utter
silence, endeavoring to stifle their breathing. Then Thandar
heard a cautious movement upon the opposite side of the
room. Was it his foe, or Nadara? He raised his pistol level
with a man's breast, and then very cautiously he too moved
to one side. At the sound of his movement there came a
sudden flash and deafening roar from across the hut — the
enemy had fired, and in the flash of his gun all within the
interior was lighted for an instant, and to the man's left stood
Nadara, safe from a shot from Thandar's pistol.

The black, not knowing that Thandar was armed, had not
guessed that his chance shot was to prove his own death
messenger. The instant that the flash of the other's gun
revealed his whereabouts Thandar's pistol gave an answering
roar, and simultaneously Thandar leaped to one side, running
swiftly to grapple with the black from the other side; but when
he came to him, instead of meeting with ferocious resistance
as he had expected, he stumbled over his dead body.

But now the whole camp was awake. The pirates were
running hither and thither shouting questions and order in
their many tongues. Confusion reigned supreme, and in the

midst of it Thandar grasped Nadara's hand and ran from the hut. Back of the other huts he ran until he had passed the end of the camp. Then he turned down toward the water. It was his intention to reach a boat and make his way to the *Priscilla*.

Behind them the confusion of the camp grew as the pirates searched the huts for an explanation of the two shots — there could have been no better opportunity for escape. Drawn up on the beach was one of the *Priscilla's* own boats. Together Thandar and Nadara pushed it off, and a moment later were rowing rapidly toward the yacht.

It was with a feeling of unbounded security and elation that Waldo Emerson clambered over the side and drew Nadara after him; but his elation was short lived for scarcely had he set foot upon the deck than he was seized from behind by half a dozen brawny villains who had been upon guard on board the *Priscilla* and had seen the two put off from shore, watched their flight toward the yacht and lain in wait for them as they clambered over the side.

The balance of the night they were kept prisoners upon the *Priscilla*; but early the next morning they were taken ashore. There they found all the pirates congregated outside one of the huts. Within were the passengers and crew of the *Priscilla*. As Thandar and Nadara approached they were seized and hustled toward the doorway — with an accompaniment of oriental oaths they were pushed into the interior.

Standing about in disconsolate and unhappy groups were the crew of the *Priscilla*. Captain Burlinghame and Mr. and Mrs. Smith-Jones. As his eyes fell upon the last, Waldo Emerson ran to her with outstretched arms.

With a horrified shriek Mrs. Smith-Jones dodged behind her husband and the captain. Waldo came to a sudden halt. The two men eyed him threateningly. He looked straight into his father's face.

"Don't you know me, Father?" he asked.

John Alden Smith-Jones' jaw dropped.

"Waldo Emerson," he cried. "It cannot be possible!"

Mrs. Smith-Jones emerged from retreat.

"Waldo Emerson!" she echoed. "It cannot be!"

"But it is, Mother," cried the young man.

"What awful apparel!" said Mrs. Smith-Jones after she had embraced her son. Then her eyes wandered to Nadara, who had been standing in demure silence just within the doorway.

"You?" she gasped. "You are not dead?"

Nadara shook her head, and Waldo Emerson hastened to recount her adventures since Stark's attack upon her on the deck of the *Priscilla.* Mrs. Smith-Jones approached the girl. She placed a hand upon her shoulder.

"I have been doing a great deal of thinking since last I saw you," she said, "and the result of it is that I am going to do something I have never done in my life — I am going to ask your pardon; I treated you shamefully. I do not need to ask if my son loves you — you have already told me that you love him — and his eyes have told me where his heart lies.

"For long nights I lay awake thinking of the horror of it, and almost praying that he might be dead rather than come back to find you waiting for him in Boston — that was before you went overboard. You had no birth or family, and that to me meant everything; but since I thought you were both dead I discovered that I recalled many things about you that were infinitely to be preferred over birth and breeding.

"I cannot tell you just what they are — only I cannot blame my son for loving you. Only you must discard that horrible garment for something presentable."

"Mother!" shouted Waldo Emerson, as he threw his arms about her. "I knew that you would love her, too, if you ever knew her."

Just then the door opened and one of the pirates entered.

"Come," he said.

They filed out past him. From those outside they learned that it had been decided to kill them all and after looting the *Priscilla,* sinker, as a man-of-war had been sighted cruising off the coast early in the morning. In their terror they had decided to wait no longer for the absent chief, and all thoughts of ransom were forgotten in the made desire to erase every vestige of their piracy.

The victims looked at one another in horror. They were entirely surrounded by the pirates, and one by one were securely bound that there might be no chance of any escaping. The plan was to lead them inland to the densest part of the

jungle and there to cut their throats and leave their corpses
for the vultures. The pirates seemed to derive much pleasure
in recounting their plan to the prisoners.

At last all were bound and the death march commenced.
The last of the long line of hope forsaken prisoners and
brutal, gibing cutthroats had disappeared in the jungle when
a rude craft made its way into the harbor. At sight of the
Priscilla it hesitated and prepared to fly, but seeing no sign of
life aboard it, approached, and finding the decks deserted,
mounted. In the cabins the newcomers discovered two Malays
asleep. These they woke with much laughter and rude jests.

The two guards leaped to their feet, feeling for their pistols;
but when they saw who had surprised them they grinned
broadly and jabbered volubly. They addressed all their re-
marks to a huge and villainous fellow whom they called chief.
He it was whom the pirates had awaited, and whose prolonged
absence had resulted in the determination to execute the
prisoners of the *Priscilla*.

When the chief learned of what was going on in the jungle
he cursed and bellowed in rage. He saw many thousand liang
of sycee evaporating before his eyes. Shouting orders to his
fellow to follow him he leaped into the craft hat had brought
them to the *Priscilla*, and a moment later was pushing rapidly
toward the shore. Without waiting to draw the boat upon the
beach the chief plunged into the jungle, his men at his heels.

Far ahead of him trudged the weary and fear-stricken
prisoners, lashed onward by sticks and the flats of murderous
parangs. At last the pirates halted in a tangled mass of
vegetation.

"Here," said one; but another thought they should proceed
a little further. For a few minutes the two men argued, then
the first drew his parang and advanced upon Thandar.

"Here!" he insisted and swung the blade about his head.

A sudden crashing of the underbrush and loud and angry
shouts caused him to turn his eyes in the direction of the
interruption. The prisoners, too, looked. What they saw was
not particularly reassuring — only another very ferocious
appearing and exceeding wrathful pirate followed by a half
dozen other villains.

He rushed into the midst of the group, knocking men to right and left. The wicked looking fellows who had bullied and cowed the frightened prisoners but a few moments before now looked the picture of abject terror.

The chief came to a halt before the man with the bared parang. His face was livid, and working spasmodically with rage and excitement. He tried to speak, and then he turned his eyes upon Thandar, standing there bound ready for decapitation. As his gaze fell upon this prisoner his eyes went wide, and then he turned upon the would-be executioner, and with a mighty blow felled him.

That seemed to loose his tongue, and from his mouth flowed a torrent of the most awful abuse the prisoners had ever heard. It was directed toward the men who had dared contemplate this thing without his sanction, and principally against the cowering unfortunate who had not dared rise from where his chief's heavy fist had sprawled him.

"And you would have killed Thandar," he shrieked. "Thandar, who saved my life!"

And then he fell to kicking the prostrate man until Thandar himself was forced to intercede in the wretch's behalf.

With the coming of Tsao Ming the troubles of the prisoners evaporated in thin air, for when he found that the owner of the *Priscilla* was Thandar's father he restored the yacht and all the loot that his men had taken from it to their rightful owners. Nor would he have stopped there had they permitted him to have his way, which was no less than to behead half a dozen of his unfortunate lieutenants who had been over-zealous in the performance of their piratical duties.

Taso Min's picturesque villains replenished the water casks of the *Priscilla* and carried aboard a plentiful table to reach Honolulu, the port they had chosen as their first stop.

And when the preparations were completed a dozen piratical prahus escorted the white yacht a hundred miles upon her northward journey, firing a farewell salute with volley after volley from the little brass six-pounders in their bows.

As the tiny fleet diminished to mere specks astern, disappearing beneath the southern horizon, a white flannelled man with close-cropped blonde hair, and a slender, black haired girl in simple shirt waist and duck suit watched them from the deck of the *Priscilla.*

And involuntary sigh escaped the lips of each and they turned and looked into one another's eyes.

XIII

HOMEWARD BOUND

*A*t Honolulu Waldo Emerson Smith-Jones and Nadara were married. Before the ceremony there had been some discussions to what name should be used in describing Nadara in the formal contract.

"Nadara" alone seemed too brief and meaningless to the precise Mrs. Smith-Jones; but Waldo Emerson and the girl insisted that it was her name and all-sufficient. So, in lieu of another name, it was finally decided by all that "Nadara" could not be legally improved upon.

Prior to the ceremony, which took place on board the *Priscilla,* Mr. and Mrs. John Alden Smith-Jones, Captain Cecil Burlinghame, several invited guests from amongst officials and friends in Honolulu, and the crew of the *Priscilla* presented gifts to the bride.

Captain Burlinghame in presenting his proffered a few words in explanation of it.

"To you, Nadara," he said, "these trinkets will hold a deeper meaning and greater value than to another, for they come from your own forgotten island where they lay for twenty years until, by chance, I picked them up close by the sea. The poor lady to whom they once belonged you never knew — it is quite possible that she was never upon your savage coast — and how her jewels came to be there must always remain a mystery. But two things you hold in common with her, for she was a lady and she was very beautiful."

He held toward Nadara in his open palm a little worn bag of skins of small rodents, sewn together with bits of gut. At sight of it both the girl and Waldo Emerson exclaimed in astonishment.

Nadara took the bag wonderingly in her hands and dumped the contents into her palm. Waldo pressed forward.

"Did you know to whom these belonged?" he asked Burlinghame.

"To Eugénie Marie Céleste de la Valois, Countess of Cercy," replied the captain.

"They belonged to Nadara's mother," returned Waldo. "Her foster parents were present at her birth and took these jewels from the poor woman's body after she had passed away. She was washed ashore in a boat in where there was only a dead man beside herself — Nadara was born that night."

And so, when the clergyman had performed the marriage ceremony he entered upon the certificate in the space provided there for the name of the woman: Nadara de la Valois.

And they are living in Boston now in a wonderful home that you have seen if you ever have been to Boston and been driving about in one of those great sight-seeing motor busses, for the place is pointed out to all visitors because of the beauty of its architecture and fame that attaches to the historic and aristocratic name of its owner, which, as it happens, is not Smith-Jones at all.

www.ingramcontent.com/pod-product-compliance
Lightning Source LLC
Chambersburg PA
CBHW050805250626
47155CB00005B/2213